A VIRGIN
FOR A VOW

BY
MELANIE MILBURNE

MILLS
BOON

First Published in Great Britain 2017
By Mills & Boon, an imprint of HarperCollins*Publishers*
1 London Bridge Street, London, SE1 9GF

© 2017 Melanie Milburne

ISBN: 978-0-263-93397-0

Printed and bound in Spain
by CPI, Barcelona

more tempting than she wanted to admit. 'I promise.'

'Oh, and one other thing,' he warned. 'I might be standing in for someone who doesn't exist, but that's as far as your little fantasy goes. Understood?'

'I hope you're not thinking I'd want you to actually *marry* me, because that's just utterly ridiculous!'

'Go...
you

...kissing him, which was even...herself

...ance to...
...burne

...Medallion—a prestigious
...rary talent.

...walks in the Tasmanian bush.
...Foundation and a keen dog lover
...n. Melanie is an ambassador for
...novel, and thus her career as a
...leting a master's degree in education,

Please return/renew this item by the last date shown to avoid a charge. Books may also be renewed by phone and Internet. May not be renewed if required by another reader.

www.libraries.barnet.gov.uk

BARNET
LONDON BOROUGH

Melanie Milb...

the age of seven... exams. After comp... she decided to write a... romance author was bo... the Australian Childhood... and trainer. She enjoys long... In 2015 Melanie won the Holt... award honouring outstanding lite...

Books by Melanie Mil...

Mills & Boon Modern Rom...

The Tycoon's Marriage Deal
The Temporary Mrs Marchetti
Unwrapping His Convenient Fiancée
His Mistress for a Week
At No Man's Command

One Night With Consequences
A Ring for the Greek's Baby

Wedlocked!
Wedding Night with Her Enemy

The Ravensdale Scandals
Ravensdale's Defiant Captive
Awakening the Ravensdale Heiress
Engaged to Her Ravensdale Enemy
The Most Scandalous Ravensdale

The Playboys of Argentina
The Valquez Bride
The Valquez Seduction

Visit the Author Profile page
at millsandboon.co.uk for more titles.

A VIRGIN
FOR A VOW

To my previous editor, Flo Nicoll.

It was wonderful working with you on
so many books. You encouraged me, supported me
and challenged me to constantly lift my writing.

I will never forget meeting you in person in Sydney.
Nor will I forget all the funny conversations
we've had over thirty-plus books.

Bless you for being wonderful you. xxxx

CHAPTER ONE

ABBY HAD ONE day left to respond to the invitation to the ball. One day. Twenty-four hours. Fourteen hundred and forty minutes. Eighty-six thousand and four hundred seconds. And if she didn't come up with a 'fiancé' by then she was toast.

Burned and charred and utterly useless toast.

She sat at her desk and stared at the gold and black vellum invitation with its fancy copperplate writing.

Miss Abby Hart and Fiancé

Panic knocked on her heart like a boxer's fist, threatening to punch it right out the back of her chest. She couldn't show up at *Top Goss and Gloss's* prestigious Spring Charity Ball alone. It was the biggest event on her career calendar. There was a three-to four-year waiting list for tickets. There were more senior people on staff than her who had never received an invitation. Receiving a personalised invitation from the head honcho as 'guest of honour' was a big deal. A seriously big deal. Declining the invitation was out of the question. Her boss insisted it was time for Abby's adoring fans to finally meet her fiancé. If she showed up at the ball alone she might as well take her resignation with her instead.

Everyone thought Abby was engaged to her childhood sweetheart. Everyone at work. Everyone online. Everyone on the flipping planet thought she was engaged. But she didn't have a childhood sweetheart. She hadn't even had a proper childhood. Not unless you could call being shunted in and out of foster homes since you were five years old a childhood.

'Abby, have you got time for a—? Hey, haven't you sent your RSVP for the ball yet? Wasn't the deadline like a week ago?' Sabina from Fashion asked with a frown.

Abby posted an *everything's cool* smile on her face. 'I know but I'm still waiting to hear back from my fiancé about it. He...he is super-busy with work stuff just now and—'

'But surely he's taking you to the ball?' Sabina said. 'I mean, that's what a fiancé does, right? This is the night everyone finally gets to meet your mysterious Mr Perfect. That's why the ball has been such a massive sell-out. I think it's so cool how you always call him that in your column and blog. You've created such a mystery about his identity. It's like it's London's best-kept secret.'

Abby had only been able to keep his identity a secret because Mr Perfect had no identity. He didn't exist other than in her imagination. Her weekly blog and column was all about relationships. Dating advice. About finding and keeping true love. Helping people find their own happy-ever-after. She had hundreds of thousands of readers and millions of followers on Twitter who wrote in for her advice.

Gulp.

Yes, millions.

Who all thought she was happily engaged to her own perfect man. She even wore an engagement ring to prove it. Not a bona fide diamond but a zirconia, which was so darn realistic no one had noticed it wasn't the real deal and she'd been wearing it for the last two and a half years.

'Oh, no, he would never let me down.' It sometimes scared her how good she was at lying.

'I wish I'd been invited to the ball,' Sabina said with a sigh that Cinderella would have been proud of. 'I'm absolutely dying to meet him. I'm sure that's why you got the invitation to sit at the boss's table. Everyone wants to meet this amazingly romantic guy who puts every other man out there to shame.'

Abby kept her smile in place but her stomach was churning so fast she could have provided enough butter for a shortbread factory. Two factories. Possibly the whole of Scotland. She had to come up with a plan. She had to come up with a man.

But who?

Just then a text message pinged in on her phone from her best friend, Ella Shelverton.

Her best friend who had an older brother.

Of course! It was a brilliant solution. But would Luke want to go with her? She hadn't seen him since that night six months ago when he'd been acting a little out of character, to put it mildly. She had never been that physically close to him before. He was always a little standoffish and gruff—understandable since he was still getting over the tragic death of his girlfriend, who had been killed five years ago. But that night when Abby had called in to collect something Ella had left behind the day before, Luke had been so out of it his head had rested on her shoulder and he'd slurred his words so much she'd had to help him into his bed. Once she'd got him into bed, his hand had taken hers and for a moment she'd thought he was going to pull her down to join him, but instead he'd touched her face as if he was touching a fragile orchid and then he'd closed his eyes and promptly fallen asleep. But she could still feel the tingles in her flesh if she allowed herself to think about it.

Which she absolutely never did.

Well…only occasionally.

'Is that your fiancé texting you?' Sabina asked, leaning forward. 'What did he say? Is he coming with you?'

Abby covered the screen of her phone with her hand. 'One of Abby's rules is don't share your lover's texts with your friends. They're private.'

Sabina gave a heartfelt sigh. 'I wish I had a lover's text to share. I wish I had what you have, Abby. But then, everyone wants what you have.'

What exactly do I have?

Abby kept her expression in caring colleague

mode. 'I hate to sound like an agony aunt but that's what I am so here goes. You're a gorgeous person who deserves to be happy just like anyone else. You can't let one bad experience with a two-timing jerk—'

'Three-timing. Possibly four but I'm not sure if he was boasting about the redhead.'

'Right, yes, I forgot—three-or four-timing jerk discourage you from finding the amazing and loving and commitment-friendly man who is out there just waiting to find a wonderful girl like you,' Abby said.

Sabina smiled. 'No wonder you're London's top relationships columnist. You always have the perfect answer.'

Abby had thought long and hard but eventually decided against calling Luke before she turned up at his house in Bloomsbury. She didn't want to give him the opportunity to fob her off using the excuse of being too busy with work. He was always working on one of his medical engineering projects for which he'd become globally recognised. She'd made Ella promise not to say anything to him about her plan until she had spoken to him in person. Ella was surprisingly keen on the idea of Luke taking her to the ball when Abby had told her about it. Although, maybe it wasn't so surprising given Ella made no secret of the fact she longed for her big brother to get some sort of social life happening again.

Not that Luke was likely to answer a call from Abby even if he did have his phone on. He kept his distance from most people, but especially from her, which made his up close and personal behaviour that night all the more unusual. But the kind of conversation she had in mind would be much better done face to face.

And because she knew he was a sucker for a bit of home baking, turning up on his swanky doorstep with a box of chocolate chip and macadamia nut cookies still warm from the oven would hopefully work a treat.

Well, it would if he would jolly well answer his door.

Abby balanced the cookies under one arm and huddled under her umbrella, trying to ignore the icy spring rain spiking and splashing her ankles. She pressed the brass button for the fifth time and left it there. She knew he was home because there were lights on in his office and another one in the sitting room.

Maybe he has someone with him...
No.

She dismissed the thought out of hand. Luke hadn't had anyone with him since his girlfriend Kimberley's death five years ago. Not that he had been much of a party animal before that, but after Kimberley was killed in a car crash he became even more of a loner. He was the epitome of the locked down workaholic. It was sad because she couldn't help thinking he might be quite a fun person to be around if he let himself go a bit.

Abby finally heard the tread of firm footsteps and

took her finger off the bell just as the door opened. His frowning expression wasn't what you could even loosely call welcoming. 'Oh, it's you…' he said.

'Nice to see you too, Luke,' Abby said. 'Can I come in? It's kind of wet and cold out here.'

'Sure,' he said while his expression clearly said an emphatic no.

Abby blithely ignored that, stepping over the threshold and folding her umbrella, which unfortunately sent a spray of water droplets on to the plush carpet runner that was threatening to swallow her up to her knees. Maybe even up to her neck. 'Have I called at a bad time?'

'I'm working on something—'

'There are more things in life than work, you know,' Abby said, hunting around for somewhere to place her umbrella.

'Here.' He held out his hand with a long-suffering look. 'I'll take that before you take out a window.'

Abby gave him the squinty eye. 'I *am* house-trained. It's just your house is always so darn perfect it makes me feel like I'm walking into a *Vogue Living* set.'

He took the umbrella and placed it on a stand near the door, somehow without allowing a single droplet of water to fall. Amazing. 'Isn't Ella with you?'

'She's got a parent teacher meeting at school this evening,' Abby said. 'I thought I'd drop in by my-self. To…erm…see how you are.'

'I'm fine—as you can see.'

There was a pregnant silence. A triplets or even quads pregnant silence.

Abby wondered if he was thinking about That Night. Did he ever think about it? Did he even remember it? Did he remember touching her so gently? Resting his head on her shoulder and then cradling her cheek in his hand like he was going to kiss her?

His eyes moved between each of hers in a studying way, like an academic trying to make sense of a complicated article. He was the only one who looked at her like that. In that quiet, assessing way that made her nerves start to jangle. As if he was searching for the frightened, abandoned child she had hidden deep inside herself so many years ago.

The child no one ever saw.

No one.

'Abby.' His voice contained a note of censure. 'I'm really busy right now so—'

Abby shoved the box of cookies towards him. 'Here—I made these for you.'

He took the box like he was taking a detonating device. 'What's this for?'

'They're your favourite cookies. I made them before I came over.'

He gave a God-give-me-strength sigh and put the box down on the polished walnut hall table. He led the way to the sitting room, offering her the sofa with the wave of a hand, but he remained standing as if he had set himself a time limit on her visit. 'What do you want?'

'That's a bit rude, don't you think? Just because I call on you with your favourite cookies you immediately assume I want something in return,' Abby said, folding her arms and affecting a wounded expression that wouldn't have looked out of place on a three-year-old.

Luke's gaze went to her pouting lower lip, lingered there for a beat before coming back to mesh with hers. When those dark blue eyes locked on hers something wearing feather slippers shuffled across the floor of her belly. He cleared his throat and scraped his hand over his jaw. 'Scraped' being the operative word because the amount of stubble he had going on there was a telling reminder of the potent male hormones surging through his body. He was normally so clinically clean-shaven it was a shock to see him so ungroomed. Not a nasty shock. A pleasant I-would-like-to-see-more-of-this-side-to-him shock.

Which was kind of shocking in itself because Abby had taught herself *not* to notice Luke Shelverton. He was her best friend's older brother. It was a boundary she had sworn never to cross. But for some reason her eyes were getting a little too happy about resting on Luke's staggeringly handsome features. His sapphire-blue eyes were framed and fringed by jet-black eyebrows and lashes, but his hair was a rich dark brown and was currently ruffled as if he'd been combing it with his fingers. Broad-shouldered and lean-hipped, with an abdomen you could crack walnuts on, he was the stuff of female fantasies. He had the sort of facial and body structure that would have made Michelangelo rush off to stock up on chisels and marble.

'Look, about that night...' he said.

'I'm not here about *that* night,' Abby said. 'I'm here about another night. The most important night of my life.' She took a quick breath and let it out in a rush. 'I need you to do me a favour. I need a fiancé for one night.' There. She'd said it. She'd put it out there.

Everything on his face stilled. His entire body seemed to be snap frozen as if every muscle and ligament and corpuscle of blood had turned to stone.

Even the air seemed to be sucked right out of the room.

But then he let out a breath and walked over to a drinks cabinet. 'I'm going to pretend I didn't hear that. Would you like a drink before you go?'

Abby sat on the sofa and crossed one leg over the other as if she was settling in for the evening. No way was she leaving until she had this nailed. 'I'll have a red wine.' White wine wasn't going to cut it this time. And she certainly wasn't in the mood for champagne.

Not until she convinced Luke to help her.

Luke came over with the wine and handed it to her. Abby tried to avoid his fingers in the exchange but somehow they both let go of the glass at the same time and it landed with a blood-like splash over the front of her brand-new baby blue cotton and cashmere blend sweater. Well, it wasn't brand new—she'd bought it at a second-hand shop for a ridiculously cheap price—but it was cashmere.

'Oops!' She leapt off the sofa, almost knocking him over in her scramble to get up. But her leap sent more drops of wine splashing over the cream carpet and the sofa. 'Oh, no…'

He steadied her with two strong hands on her upper arms; the sensation of his fingers pressing into her skin even through the layers of her clothing was nothing short of electrifying. He dropped his hold as if he'd felt the same voltage, and took a clean white handkerchief from his pocket. For a moment she thought he was going to mop her breasts for her but then he seemed to collect himself and handed it to her instead. 'Don't worry about the carpet and the sofa. They've been treated with a stain resistant.' His voice was so husky it sounded like he'd been snacking on gravel.

Abby dabbed at her breasts and tried not to notice how close he was. She could smell the subtle lime notes of his aftershave and a base note of something else, something woodsy and arrantly masculine. She could even see the individual pinpoints of his regrowth on his chin, the way it was liberally sprinkled around his well sculptured mouth, making her want to press her fingertips to it to see if it felt as prickly as it looked.

She balled the soiled handkerchief into one hand while the other pulled her soaked sweater away from her breasts. 'Do you have something I could wear while I take this off and rinse it?'

'Can't you just put your coat over it or something?'

Abby blew out a breath. 'This sweater cost me a week's wages.' No way was she going to admit it was second-hand. 'And don't get me started about my bra.' Which wasn't second-hand and had cost a packet because no way was she going to wear someone else's underwear. She had done that for most of her childhood.

His frown made his forehead wrinkle like isobars on a weather map. 'Unbelievable.'

'What? Why do you say that?' Abby asked. 'I work at a fashion magazine. I have to wear the latest fashion. I can't be seen out and about in last season's threads.'

'Don't they give you freebies or a discount?'

Abby moved her gaze to the left of his. 'I'm not a fashion editor. I just write a weekly relationships column.'

'Come with me,' he said and led the way out of the room to the downstairs bathroom. 'Wait here. I'll bring you something from upstairs.'

Abby closed the bathroom door and took off the sweater. She grimaced at the state of her bra. Why had she worn the virginal white one when she could have worn the red?

Because you're a virgin?

Don't remind me.

Which made her wonder…when was the last time Luke had sex? Had he had sex with anyone since Kimberley's death? Five years was a long time to be celibate if you'd had a regular sex life before. Which Abby was pretty certain he'd had. Men as sexy as Luke Shelverton did not have to work too hard to find lovers. One look from him and women came out of the woodwork like termites.

There was a knock at the bathroom door and Abby held a hand towel across her breasts and opened the door. Luke handed her a finely woven sweater the colour of his eyes. 'I know it's too big but I don't have anything your size.'

Abby took the sweater from him and held it against her chest along with the towel. She could smell the clean scent of wool wash on the soft fibres and even a faint trace of him. 'Ella told me she thought you still had some of Kimberley's clothes.'

His eyes hardened to chips of blue ice. 'Is this scheme of stand-in fiancé something you and Ella have cooked up together?'

Abby held the sweater against her chest like armour. 'No. It was my idea but she thought it was a good plan. She said it was high time you went to something other than a boring engineering function. And since you and Ella are the only people in my life who know I'm not really engaged, in a way you're the only one who can help me.'

'What about your family? Don't they know?'

Family. That was another thing Abby had done some considerable embellishing over. She hadn't even told Ella the truth about her background. Abby didn't have a family. She didn't want her friends, much less her adoring public, to know she had grown up in numerous foster homes with a bunch of other needy kids and overworked, overwrought, overbearing at times foster parents. The last family she'd stayed with had been the most functional, but even they hadn't kept in touch with her once she'd left the foster system.

Even Abby's surname was a stage name because she had more skeletons in her closet than she had clothes. She didn't want anyone putting her real surname in a search engine and linking her to a now deceased drug-addicted prostitute and a man currently in jail for assault with a deadly weapon. She couldn't bear reliving the shame all over again. Being reminded she had never been loved as a child should be loved, never protected as a child should be protected.

Never wanted.

There were some things you just had to keep private.

Abby couldn't quite meet Luke's gaze. 'Of course they know. But it's not like they can do anything. You're the only one I can ask to do this.'

'I'm sorry, Abby. You'll have to find someone else.'

Abby forgot about covering her wine-splashed bra and handed him back his sweater. 'Look, Luke, I know the last five years have been tough on you, really tough, but don't you ever want to just go out and have a night on the town like normal people do?'

His eyes flicked to her bra-covered breasts and then returned to hold her gaze in a steely blue trap.

'What's normal about pretending to millions of people you're in a relationship that doesn't even exist?'

Abby grabbed her sweater from the marble basin console and pulled it back over her head, thrusting her arms through the sleeves with such force she nearly tore a hole in one of them. 'I'll tell you what's normal,' she said, popping her head out of the collar to glare at him, not caring that her wavy hair was as ruffled and wild as her temper. 'It's normal to help friends out when they're in a pickle. But you keep pushing all your friends away since Kimberley died, which is so sad because your friends and family are who you need to get you through this. You're needed, Luke. Ella and your mum need you and I do too.'

His mouth was so tightly set a postage stamp couldn't have been pushed between his lips. 'I think you've said enough.'

No way had Abby said enough. She wasn't going to be put off her plan. She had to get him to agree to it.

She *had* to.

'My entire career is at stake here. I can't go to the ball without a partner. I'm supposed to be half of one of London's most influential couples. I'll be fired on the spot if they find out I've made him up. I want so much to raise funds for this charity. It's my way to really make a difference in the world. There'll be sponsors there who are going to pay hundreds, possibly thousands of pounds to see me there with my fiancé. You have to help me, Luke. You have to go with me. You have to!'

He slowly shook his head at her as if she were a child having a tantrum, his arms folded across his chest, his feet firmly planted like centuries-old tree trunks. 'No.'

Desperation was climbing up Abby's spine like hundreds of faceless creatures with hooked claws. So many people would be at that ball. Important people. Stars, celebrities, movers and shakers and even minor royalty. Possibly major royalty. Maybe the Queen would be there—she'd turned up at the Olympics, so why not the Spring Ball?

People were expecting to see Abby there with her fiancé. It was unthinkable for her to be there on her own. Her chance to do her bit for disadvantaged kids like her would be ruined if she didn't show up on the arm of her soulmate. The thought of those poor little kids missing out on the things she had missed out on because her fundraising attempt had blown up in her face was heartbreaking.

Why couldn't Luke do this one small thing for her?

Abby stalked past him out of the bathroom and went back to the sitting room, where she had left her bag and phone. 'Right, well, then. I thought you were a friend but clearly I'm mistaken about that.'

His expression showed no trace of emotion. 'Your sweater is on back to front.'

Abby looked down at her sweater and suppressed a groan. Why was she always so clumsy and gauche around him? It hardly helped her cause to be acting like a clown in a farce. She put her phone down and drew her arms out of the sleeves while still wearing the sweater and turned it around so it was facing the right way before poking her arms back through the sleeves. 'There. Happy now, Mr Perfect?'

Mr Perfect?

His eyes dropped to her mouth but then just as quickly jerked back to her eyes as if he was fighting some inner demon and only just winning the battle. 'Why didn't you say anything to Ella about that night?'

'How do you know I didn't tell her?'

'She would've mentioned it by now if you had.'

Abby let out a long breath. 'I didn't want her to know you were drowning your sorrows in booze. She worries about you enough as it is.'

He looked taken aback. 'I wasn't drunk...' He paused for a beat. 'I had a migraine.'

'A migraine?' Abby frowned. 'But there was an empty wine glass on—'

'I'd had one drink after work but it triggered a migraine. I get them occasionally.'

Did his sister and mother know about his migraines? Did anybody know? Abby couldn't stop her gaze from darting to his mouth and back again. Had it been wishful thinking on her part to think he had almost kissed her? Had she *wanted* him to kiss her?

Damn right she had.

'Do you remember anything about that night?' Abby said. 'Anything at all?'

'Not much.' His tone had an edge of something

she couldn't quite identify. 'I didn't…do or say anything to you that I shouldn't have, did I?'

She couldn't control the impulse to send her tongue over lips that suddenly felt drier than the carpet she was standing on. His gaze followed every millimetre of the journey, leaving a trail of blistering, tingling heat along the entire surface of her lips as if his mouth and not his eyes had rested there. 'You mean like make a pass at me?'

A flicker of worry flashed over his face. 'Please tell me I didn't.'

'Maybe if you kissed me again you'd remember if you did or not.'

Are you completely and utterly crazy?

Abby had no idea why she'd issued such a daring challenge but it popped out of her mouth and was now hovering in the air between them like an intoxicating vapour.

Or maybe she did know why she'd said it—because she wanted him to kiss her. Had wanted it ever since that night.

A real kiss.

Not an almost one.

She couldn't pull her gaze away from his mouth, or pull her mind away from the thought of his firm disapproving lips pressing down on hers. Wondering how his mouth would feel—hard or soft or somewhere deliciously in between. How he would taste—salty with a hint of coffee or mint or maybe even a lick of top-shelf brandy. She was getting tipsy on the images her mind was spinning—images of him taking her by the shoulders and pulling her against his broad chest and plundering her mouth with his.

Yes, plundering, like one of those swashbuckling heroes in the period dramas she loved to watch on rainy Sunday afternoons.

Luke stepped closer and placed his hand beneath her chin, his fingers warm and firm against her skin. She couldn't remember him ever touching her before, apart from That Night, but the same thing happened now. Nerves she didn't know she possessed leapt and danced and all but fainted at his touch. The space between their bodies pulsated with magnetic energy—energy that rippled in the air like an invisible current.

His eyes held hers in a searing tether that made something in her core quiver and a shiver rolled down her spine like a runaway firecracker. This close she could see every thick lash fringing his mesmerising lapis lazuli eyes, the way his pupils were black and wide like bottomless pools of ink. She could see the detailed sculpture of his mouth, the deep philtrum ridge and the well-defined vermillion borders, and wondered again what it would feel like to have those lips clamped to hers.

'Read my lips.' His voice was so firm it sounded as if it was underlined. In bold and italics for good measure. 'I am not going to the ball. Got it?'

Abby was more than reading his lips. She was studying them as if she was swotting for a final exam. Had she ever seen a more gorgeous mouth? Not that it was a mouth that ever smiled. She couldn't remember the last time she'd seen him crack a grin. But then, his air of brooding gravitas had always secretly fascinated her.

Abby had to get him to change his mind about the ball. She had to. Had to. Had to. Her career depended on it. Her reputation. The children at risk charity she was raising funds for would not reach its target if she didn't show up with a fiancé in tow.

She blew out a breath and cast him a shamefaced glance from beneath her lashes. 'Okay, so I might have misled you a bit about that night. You didn't kiss me. You didn't even try but—'

'Then why did you let me think I had?' Luke dropped his hand from her face and frowned as if he was doing it for *The Guinness Book of Records*.

Abby's cheeks were feeling so hot she thought she might end up with a world record herself. 'I don't know...'

'You don't know?' His voice had a razor-sharp edge to it that nicked at her nerves.

She bit down on her lip. 'I guess I was a bit shocked when I found you so out of it that night. I stupidly jumped to conclusions and assumed you were drunk.'

'But why mislead me to believe I made a pass at you if I didn't even touch you?'

'Actually, you did touch me.'

His eyes flared as if her words shocked him to the core. 'Where did I...?' He left the question hanging in the air.

'You put your arm around my waist when I helped

you into bed,' Abby said. 'And you rested your head on my shoulder and looked at me kind of like you were thinking about kissing me.' She couldn't bring herself to mention the way he'd stroked her face.

'There's a big difference between thinking and doing.'

Abby looked up into his frowning gaze and blinked back the sting of tears. She'd taught herself not to cry over the years but she was scarily close to breaking point. 'Please, Luke, don't make me beg. I'm really sorry about my little white lie. I shouldn't have made you think you'd almost kissed me. But I have a lot riding on this ball. It's just one night and then it will be over and I won't ask you to do another thing for me ever again. I promise.'

'Why's the ball such a big deal? Isn't it just another one of your show pony parties?'

Show pony parties? Was that how he saw her? As some shallow little party hopper with nothing better to do than have a spray tan and get a manicure? Which reminded her—she had to get a spray tan and a manicure. 'I know my career must seem ridiculously vacuous to a nerdy engineer like you, but I happen to love working at a gossip magazine and tomorrow night is the biggest fundraising event of the year,' Abby said. 'There's a silent auction as well as a live auction and amazing lucky door prizes worth thousands of pounds and a dinner cooked by celebrity chefs to raise funds for a children at risk charity. The ball has a three-to four-year waiting list for tickets. I can't not go because my boss will fire

me when she finds out I've been pretending to be engaged all along. And I especially can't show up without my other half since we were nominated as one
of this year's most popular and influential couples.'

His frown was a deep trench between his night
sky eyes. 'You're going to have to tell everyone eventually you aren't in a relationship.'

Abby knew she would have to announce some sort
of breakup eventually, but how much easier would
that be if Luke stood in as her fiancé at the ball?
She could even blog and tweet breakup tips once
the ball was out of the way. The thought of telling
everyone that she, the relationships expert, was single and still a virgin was not something she wanted
to do in a hurry—if ever. 'But don't you see? I need
a stand-in fiancé in order to break up with him. I'll
find someone for myself eventually. Maybe I'll try
one of those dating apps. But I have to get through
the ball first.'

He did an I-can't-believe-you're-for-real eye-roll
and made a move to the sitting room door, holding
it open in a pointed manner. 'If you'll excuse me, I
have some work to get back to.'

Abby knew this was her last chance to get him to
change his mind. 'Please, please, *please* do this for
me, Luke. Just for a couple of hours. You can leave
early—no one will suspect anything. Think of all
those poor little disadvantaged kids you'll be helping. You will literally be changing their lives by pretending to be my fiancé for two hours.'

He kept looking at her without speaking for so

long she began to mentally dictate her resignation letter. But then he released a long and weighted sigh. 'All right—you win. I'll take you for two hours, tops. But you have to accept this is a one-off occasion and it will *not* be repeated.'

Abby was flooded with such a tide of relief she had to stop from flinging herself into his arms and hugging him. Or kissing him, which was even more tempting than she wanted to admit. 'Okay. Okay. Of course. I only need you for one night. I promise.'

They briefly discussed arrangements about Luke picking her up and what to wear and then he walked her to the front door of his house. 'One other thing,' he said.

Abby glanced up at him. 'Yes?'

He seemed to be having some trouble keeping his gaze away from her mouth. It kept tracking back to it as if programmed to do so. 'I might be standing in for someone who doesn't actually exist but that's as far as your little fantasy goes. Understood?'

Abby wondered what he meant by such a comment. 'I hope you're not thinking I'd want you to actually marry me because that's just utterly ridiculous.'

'Good to know,' he said. 'See you tomorrow, Cinderella.'

CHAPTER TWO

LUKE CLOSED THE door after Abby left and let out a curse so blue he was mildly surprised to find the walls of his hallway were still white. Damn that girl. How had she got him to say yes? Had she cast some sort of spell on him? Why had he agreed to such a charade? He didn't do balls. He didn't do parties. He didn't even do dinners unless work required it of him.

And he definitely didn't date.

Since Kimberley's death he'd had no motivation to date. He felt the urge now and again but he just as quickly squashed it. He was a bad bet when it came to relationships. He had tried with Kimberley. And tried damn hard because with his father playing musical partners like some sort of born-again playboy, Luke had wanted to prove to himself he wasn't cut from the same cloth. But, for all his efforts to be a good partner, his relationship with Kimberley had floundered and he'd called time on it. He hadn't felt ready to take their relationship to the next level. Kimberley had stayed overnight several times a week and had even left some clothes and toiletries at his house, but he hadn't been willing for her to move in with him permanently. It had seemed *too* much of a commitment. Back then he hadn't been against marriage, he'd seen it as something he might do one day with the right person, yet over time it had become obvious Kimberley wasn't the right person.

But within hours of him ending their relationship Kimberley was dead.

The thought of a new relationship made him feel claustrophobic. Like someone was wrapping him in steel cords, pulling them tighter and tighter and tighter until he couldn't breathe. He couldn't think of the word commitment without his chest seizing.

But helping Abby with her little problem... Well, it had been rather nice of her to make sure he was okay that night six months ago, and he was grateful she hadn't sent his mother and sister into a fit of panic over him 'drinking' by telling them about it. Abby had come on her own to pick up something Ella had left behind the day before. He wished he could remember more about that night, but Kimberley's birthday was always hard and it always triggered a migraine. Always. He'd come home from Kimberley's parents' house, where they'd had a cake complete with candles. Even presents she'd never open.

They always invited him and he always went out of respect. Out of duty.

Out of guilt.

There was a part of him that wished he hadn't opened the door to Abby that night. He'd only been home half an hour and he'd had half a glass of wine—*foolish, he knew*—to try and ease the tension behind his eyes, but then the migraine had hit him like a sledgehammer and wiped out his motherboard, so to speak.

But he could remember Abby arriving on his doorstep with a sunny smile and those amazingly bright and clear toffee-brown eyes looking up at him like a cute spaniel.

And her mouth.

He had no trouble remembering her mouth. He could be in an induced coma for a century and still be aware of it. Dear God, what was it about her mouth? It never failed to pull his gaze to its plump fullness. It never failed to make him fantasise about how those luscious lips would feel under his. Damn it. It made him think of sex. With her.

Which was downright wrong given she was his kid sister's best friend.

That was a line he wasn't going to cross. There were some things you didn't do, and that was definitely one of them. That was, if he was actually interested in having a relationship with anyone, which he wasn't.

Not again.

He didn't want the responsibility of someone else's emotional upkeep. How could he ever relax in a relationship after being blindsided by Kimberley's tragic end? Even though he hadn't loved her, it didn't mean he didn't deeply regret her passing. Every day since he'd thought of all the things she was missing out on, the things her family were missing out on. Nothing he could say or do would ever make up for their loss.

He couldn't do that to another person, to another family. He was better out of the dating game so there was no possibility of anyone getting hurt.

But what was he going to do about Abby?

One of the little flashes of memory Luke had of that night was Abby's chestnut hair tickling his face when he leaned his pounding head against her shoulder. Her hair smelt of spring flowers. Her touch... He couldn't remember if she'd touched him first or if he'd touched her...

But no matter. The crucial thing was he remembered how it felt. It was the same feeling he had when he'd touched her face earlier. Her skin was as soft as the petal of a magnolia bloom. Her nose had a cute dusting of tiny freckles over the bridge that reminded him of chocolate sprinkled on the top of a cappuccino.

He might not have kissed her that night but he'd sure as hell wanted to. He remembered all too clearly. How could he forget a mouth like that, migraine or not? He'd thought about that mouth for the last six months. Thought and fantasised about holding Abby in his arms, touching her, kissing her.

And, yes, God strike him down, making love to her.

Luke wasn't sure why he'd finally agreed to be her stand-in fiancé. Well, maybe he did know. Seeing Abby's tears had triggered something in him. Worry that she would do something. Something silly and reckless that would destroy...

He pulled away from the thought. No, Abby wasn't like Kimberley. Abby was pragmatic and resourceful and resilient in a way Kimberley hadn't been. Abby's tears were understandable given the ball was a big deal for her. It was two hours of his time and he surely owed her that since her Florence Nightingale act six months ago.

Two hours pretending to be Abby's Mr Perfect.

How hard could it be?

Abby was trying to pull up her zip at the back of her ball gown when she heard Luke arrive at her flat the night of the ball. She gathered the back of her dress in one hand and shuffled out of her bedroom to answer the front door. She hadn't seen Luke in black tie before. Even in casual clothes he was traffic-stopping gorgeous. But in formal attire he would have stopped air traffic. Possibly even a space shuttle. At take-off.

He was certainly stopping her breath. She had to swallow a couple of times to get her voice to work. 'H...hi. I'm having some trouble with this zip. Do you think you could give me a hand?'

'Sure.' He stepped inside and closed the door. 'Turn around.'

Abby held her breath as his fingers drew the zip up her back, the gentle brush of his knuckles on her bare skin sending a shiver shimmying down her spine and straight into her lady land. Secretly fizzing and smouldering there like an ignited wick. She could feel the tall frame of his body within half a step of hers, triggering her hormones like they had never been triggered before. It was as if her body recognised something in his—something deeply primal and elemental. Her senses were singing like a mezzo-soprano in the Royal Albert Hall. If she so much as leaned back she could be flush against his chest and hips and…other things.

Male things.

But the zip would only go to a certain point.

'There's a bit of fabric caught up in the mechanism,' Luke said and continued working on it, bending over so his warm breath as well as his fingers brushed over her skin.

She suppressed a shiver and breathed in so he could gain better access, at the same time breathing in his aftershave, this time lemon and lime and a faint trace of bergamot with an understory of country leather. She couldn't stop thinking of his hands going lower, dipping down to the curve of her bottom, caressing her, shaping her, slipping his fingers between her legs…

Finally the zip moved all the way up and Luke stepped back. 'That's done it.'

That's done it all right. Abby hadn't felt so turned on in her life. She turned around and hoped her wicked thoughts were not painted bright red on her face. But it certainly felt like it. If she didn't stop blushing soon she'd be able to turn the heating down. Or off. 'Erm… I have something else for you to do… I'll just get it from my bedroom.'

Abby came back out with the fake diamond pendant she wanted to wear and handed it to him. It was a very good fake. You could hardly tell the difference. Hardly. 'The catch is so tiny I can never do it up by myself.'

Luke trailed the fine chain over his fingers, his narrowed gaze examining the 'diamond.' 'Who bought you this?'

'You did.'

His brows came together. 'When did I ever—?'

'Not you as in *you*,' Abby said. 'You as in Mr Perfect. My fiancé.'

His expression seemed to suggest he thought a white van and a straitjacket might be handy right about now. 'Are you serious? You actually buy stuff and pretend it's from someone who doesn't exist, other than in your imagination?'

'So? It's all for a good cause,' Abby said. 'I help people. It's what I do. I help them have better love lives.'

'While presumably having no love life of your own.' There was a dry edge to his tone.

'Like you can talk.' Abby turned around rather than face his piercing gaze. She had her hair in an up-do that gave him free access to her neck but even so every fine hair reacted to the presence of his fingers with tingles and shivers that went straight to her core.

'How do you know I don't have a love life?' she said, turning back around once the necklace was in place. 'I might have dozens of secret lovers stashed away.'

'None of whom you've managed to convince to take you to the ball.' He shrugged at her beady look. 'Just saying.'

Abby wasn't going to go into the details of why she'd got to the age of twenty-three without having dated regularly or had sex with anyone. Even Ella didn't know the full story. How could she tell her best friend her mother was a heroin-addicted prostitute? And that hearing her mother service her clients in the next room—and in the same room when she had been under three—had seriously messed with Abby's sexual development? She had only been kissed a couple of times and had called a halt before anyone could get any closer. She even wondered if she was frigid.

'I would have dated someone well before this but I got the job at the magazine, which, quite frankly, I didn't expect in a million squillion years to get,' Abby said. 'I was the least qualified candidate but somehow they chose me. I wrote my first couple of columns about my childhood sweetheart and somehow the readers assumed he actually existed. And then because they loved hearing about him so much I had to keep running with it.'

'How long have you worked at the magazine?'

'Two and a half years.'

His frown hadn't left his forehead but was now even deeper. 'You've been pretending for two and a half years that you're—?'

'I know it sounds crazy. It probably *is* crazy but

I wanted that job so much and I was prepared to do anything to get it.'

'Anything?'

Abby did a little lip chew. 'Well, maybe not anything, but pretending to be engaged to a guy who ticks all the boxes wasn't that hard. I mean, guys like that must exist, right? People do get married and live happily-ever-after.'

'Just as many end up in the divorce courts.'

'Just because your parents went through a hideous divorce when you were a teenager doesn't mean—'

'If we don't get going soon your two hours will be up before we even get to the ball,' Luke said, tinkling his car keys, his look more forbidding than a Keep Out sign on an army-training minefield.

Abby picked up her wrap from the back of the sofa where she'd left it earlier. She wrapped it around her shoulders, refusing to be daunted by the boxed up set to his features. 'If Kimberley hadn't died would you two have got married?'

'Abby.' His voice was like a stop sign.

'I'm sorry. Am I being pushy? I just wondered how long you dated.'

His lips were pressed almost flat. 'Three years.'

'Did you ever discuss it? Marriage, I mean?'

A muscle flickered near his mouth like a faulty switch during a power surge. 'Look, do you want me to take you to this damn ball or not?'

Abby hadn't worked in journalism for nothing. She had been known to get blood out of stones before. Whole litres of it. It was a trick of hers to get people talking about themselves so she didn't have to share anything about herself. 'Were you in love with her?'

He opened the front door and jerked his head towards the exit. 'Out.' His eyes were dark and brooding with bottled-up anger. Anger or something else...

Abby shifted her lips from side to side in a musing manner. 'Are you angry with me or at life in general? Grief can do that to—'

'Don't play the amateur psychologist with me,' he said. 'Save it for those foolish enough to fall for it.'

'I'm sensing a little resistance from you on the subject of your relationship with—'

'I wasn't in love with her, okay?' He took a deep breath as if to calm himself, one of his hands rubbing over his face like he wanted to erase something. 'And no, I wasn't going to marry her.'

'But you still miss her.'

He gave a movement of his lips that was closer to a grimace than anything near a smile. 'She was a nice young woman. She didn't deserve to have her life cut short.'

Abby touched his arm. 'I'm sure she wouldn't mind if you moved on with your life. You don't have to grieve for her for ever.'

The way he looked at her made her insides suddenly quiver. 'Are you offering yourself as a replacement?'

Abby dropped her hand from his arm as if it had been scorched. 'Of course not. You're not my type.'

'Not perfect enough for you?' There was a hint of cynicism in his tone.

'There is nothing wrong with wanting the best for yourself,' Abby said. 'Especially when you're a woman. Women often settle for second best or good enough instead of perfect. Why shouldn't we have what we want? Why should we have to compromise over something so important as a life partner?'

'So far the only perfect partner you've found is the one inside your head.'

'So far,' Abby gave a small nod. 'But I haven't given up hope yet.'

'Good luck with that.'

Luke helped Abby into his car but he was having trouble keeping his eyes away from her cleavage. The emerald-green ball gown was as sleek as a glove on her, showcasing her assets in a way that made his hormones honk and howl and do a happy dance. She wasn't super-slim but all her curves were in the right places—places he was getting hard just thinking about. The imitation diamond pendant—he knew it was an imitation because he could spot a fake a mile off—swung just above the shadowed cleft between her bra-less breasts, making him want to place his lips and tongue in that scented hollow, to taste the creamy flesh, to graze his teeth over the nipples he could see pressing against the silky fabric. The dress skimmed her waist and hips and fanned out behind her in part mermaid tail and part train. Her hair was in one of those up styles that looked like it took no time at all to do but still managed to look elegant at the same time. And it framed her face, highlighting the slope of her porcelain-smooth cheeks. Her smoky eye make-up made her brown eyes pop, but it was her mouth that kept pulling his gaze. Glistening with a shimmering lip-gloss, her Cupid's bow tortured his self-control like a yo-yo dieter at an all-you-can-eat banquet.

He had to stop drooling over her mouth.

Luke got in the driver's side of his car and curled his fingers around the steering wheel before he was tempted to reach across the console and place his hand on her silk-clad thigh. Was she even wearing knickers under that dress? The thought triggered a flare of lust so powerful it snatched his breath as if someone had grabbed him by the throat and squeezed.

Abby glanced at him. 'Are you okay?'

Luke opened and closed his fingers on the steering wheel. 'Yep.'

'You made a funny sound…kind of like you were in pain. You're not getting one of your migraines, are you?'

Now why didn't I think of that as an excuse? Not that he was the type of guy to renege on a commitment. When he made a decision he followed through on it. Two hours of his time was not a huge commitment. Thank God. 'No. Just not looking forward to making small talk. It's not my forte.'

'Don't worry, the music will be so loud you won't be able to hear yourself think.'

Which could be a very good thing given the things Luke was thinking. Things he had no business thinking. Things like how she would look without that green dress. How her gorgeous breasts would feel in his hands, in his mouth. How those sexy legs would wrap around his hips. How she would feel around him when he—

He slammed the brakes on his thoughts. He wasn't in the market for a relationship. Any sort of relationship. And Abby Hart with her happy-ever-after mission was the last person he should be thinking about. She was after the feel-good fairy tale. He still couldn't get over the fact she'd been pretending to all her readers and followers she was engaged to someone who didn't exist. Who *did* that? It took perfectionism to a whole new level. There wasn't a man on the planet who could fulfil her checklist. And he was the last man on the planet who would even try.

He wasn't going to try because he'd already been down that road and it had only ended in tragedy.

Abby began fiddling with the catch on her evening purse. 'Luke?'

'Yes?'

'There are a few things you need to know about our relationship...you know, stuff I've told my readers about you.'

Luke flicked her a glance. 'Like what?'

She nibbled at her lower lip for a moment. 'Like how you proposed.'

Shoot me now. He could just imagine what her

wacky imagination had cooked up. 'How did I—?' He couldn't even bring himself to say the word.

'You took me to Paris for the weekend and checked us into the penthouse suite of a ridiculously expensive hotel where you had organised fresh rose petals to be scattered all over the bed and flowers all over the suite,' she said. 'And you had champagne on ice and chocolate-dipped strawberries in a crystal bowl by the bed.'

'And?' Luke suspected he wasn't going to get off that lightly. Paris and champagne and strawberries and rose petals were within reason. But nothing he knew about Abby was within the realms of reason.

'We—ell...' The way she drew out the word made the back of his neck start to prickle. 'You got down on bended knee and told me I was the only one in the world for you, that you loved me more than life itself. You took out a ring box and asked me to marry you.'

Luke couldn't imagine ever saying something like that to anyone, but still.

'You had tears in your eyes,' she said. 'Lots of them. In fact, you cried. We both did because we were so happy to be—'

'Oh, for God's sake.' He made a choked-off sound. 'I can't remember the last time I cried.'

'I know some men find expressing emotion really difficult, but what about when you lost Kimberley? Didn't you cry then?'

'No.'

She gave a concerned frown. 'Oh...'

Luke had been so guilt-ridden he couldn't access

any other emotion. When he'd been told the news of Kimberley's accident he had felt completely numb. It didn't seem possible that the woman who had been in his house only a couple of hours earlier was no longer alive. He'd put the phone down after that ghastly phone call from her parents and picked up a glass where Kimberley's lipstick was still visible on the rim. How could she be dead? For the sake of her shattered family he had swung into action, helping to organise the funeral and dealing with the distressing task of informing people outside the family of her death. He had done it in an almost robotic fashion. He'd said all the right things, done all the right things, but he'd felt like there was a thick glass wall between him and the rest of the world.

It was still there.

'Her family was having enough trouble dealing with her death without me adding to their distress,' Luke said. 'I had to hold it together for them.'

He felt Abby's gaze resting on him as if she was trying to solve a Mensa puzzle. 'But what about when you were on your own? Didn't you cry then?'

'Not every person cries when sad stuff happens,' Luke said through gritted teeth. 'There are other ways to express sadness.'

'But it's really healing to have a good howl,' Abby said. 'It releases hormones and stuff. And you shouldn't be ashamed of crying just because you're a man. That's a ridiculous myth that harms men rather than helps them. Everyone should be able to cry regardless of their gender.'

Luke pulled up behind the queue of cars waiting to be parked by the valet team at the entrance of the premier hotel where the ball was being held. 'Okay, Cinderella. Anything else I should know about myself before we make an entrance?'

Her cheeks went a faint shade of pink. 'Erm... There is one other thing...'

The prickle moved from his neck to his spine. 'Go on.'

The tip of her tongue swept over her lips, making his groin tighten. 'You tell me you love me all the time. In public.'

Luke couldn't remember the last time he'd told his mother and sister he loved them, let alone anyone else. He wasn't a wordy guy. He *did* rather than *said*. His father was the opposite—lots of words and empty promises and nothing to back them up. 'O-kay.'

'And you use a lot of terms of endearment. Like honey, and baby, and sweetheart.'

That was another thing he wasn't big on, dropping cutesy endearments into every conversation. But a man had to do what a man had to do. 'Got it.'

'And we kiss. A lot.'

Luke's groin was asking for more room. Urgently. Just looking at her mouth made his blood pound and head south of the border. What would it do to him to actually kiss her? 'I'm not big on public displays of affection.'

'You are now.'

Freaking hell. What had he got himself into?

'Will you be okay with me kissing you?' Luke asked, frowning.

Her gaze kept flicking back and forth from his mouth to his eyes. 'Maybe we should have practised a bit first, you know, so we don't look stilted or awkward together.'

Now *he* couldn't stop looking at *her* mouth. Imagining how it would feel against his. 'Where do you suggest we practise? Here in the car?'

'We have time before the valet guy gets to us,' Abby said, glancing at the line of cars waiting to be parked. 'The queue is long enough.'

But was Luke's self-control strong enough? He hadn't kissed a woman in five years. Not unless he counted his mother and sister but clearly a peck on the cheek wasn't going to make the grade here. 'You really think this is necessary?'

She was already over his side of the car, her face so close to his he could feel her breath on his lips. 'Kiss me, Luke.'

Luke slid his hand along the curve of her cheek, his blood pumping so hard he could feel his erection pressing against his zip. He brought his mouth down to hers in a soft touch. *Just brush her lips and get the hell out of there.* He lifted off but her lips clung to his and something inside him gave way like tectonic plates shifting during an earthquake. He went back down again, breathing in the scent of her, relishing the fresh fruity taste of her. Her lips were soft and pillowy and tasted of strawberries or was it cherries? She made a little whimpering sound and opened to the stroke of his tongue, her tongue dancing with his, making his blood throb all the harder.

He didn't want the kiss to end. He could have kissed her all night. The feel of her lips against his, the flirty little flicker of her tongue made desire roar through his system like a rabid dog suddenly snapping its chain.

He crushed her mouth beneath his, cupping the nape of her neck so he could deepen the kiss even further. Her hands came up to link around his neck, her soft sounds of approval making everything that was male in him vibrate with fierce longing. He hadn't felt so turned on by a kiss in years. Possibly ever. Her soft mouth moulded itself to his, moving with and against his in a sexy rhythm that echoed the pulse and pound of his blood. Her perfume dazzled his senses, the luscious curves of her breasts pressed against his chest, sending a knockout blow to his self-control.

The sound of people cat-calling outside the car was the only thing that pulled Luke out of the moment. That and the flash of paparazzi cameras that were as bright and blinding as summer lightning.

Abby pulled back from him and gave a tremulous smile, her mouth slightly swollen, her cheeks flushed. 'Wow. Who would've thought?'

Right back at you, sweetheart. 'Please tell me there isn't going to be a picture of us kissing in tomorrow's tabloids,' Luke said.

She did that cute little lip chew thing again and grimaced. 'Sorry.'

CHAPTER THREE

ABBY WAS STILL trying to get her senses back under control when Luke helped her out of the car. Her mouth was tingling and so were her girly bits. Not just tingling, but aching and throbbing. She'd been kissed in the past but nothing like that. Luke's mouth had set fire to hers, making her lose all sense of time and place. But even more surprising...there hadn't been any awkwardness between them. They had kissed as if they'd been doing it for years. As if their mouths instinctively knew what the other liked.

The press surged closer and Luke put a protective arm around Abby's waist. She smiled up at him, her heart almost coming to a standstill when he smiled back. His smile made his eyes come alive in a way she had never seen before. It made him look younger, more carefree, less serious and forbidding. 'Ready?'

'Ready.' *I think.* 'Welcome to the limelight.'

The cameras were clicking so much it sounded like a round of military gunfire. And a journalist surged forward to thrust a recording device near

Abby. 'Everyone is dying to know who your Mr Perfect is. Will you introduce him to us?'

Abby smiled at the journalist. 'Sure—this is my fiancé Luke—'

'Hey—aren't you Luke Shelverton? From Shelverton Robotics?' another male journalist asked. 'You're the guy who designed that amazing technology that's revolutionised complex neurosurgery all around the world.'

Luke accepted the accolade with an on-off smile that didn't show his teeth. 'That's correct.'

'When are you two planning to get married?' the female journalist asked. 'Will we be hearing wedding bells this summer?'

Abby was still trying to think of something to say when Luke got in first. 'We're keeping the date a secret for privacy reasons,' he said.

'Do you have any dating advice from a man's perspective?' the male journalist asked.

'Just be yourself,' Luke said and began to lead Abby towards the entrance of the hotel.

But the first female journalist wasn't finished. 'What about some romance tips from London's most romantic man?'

Luke's fingers tightened on Abby's hand in an I'll-get-you-for-this-later gesture but he looked the female journalist straight in the eye. 'Look into her eyes when she's talking to you. Listen to her.'

'I'm going to use that in my next column,' Abby said when they finally got away from the press. 'Everyone is so busy on their phones these days no one ever looks at you when they're talking to you.'

'You owe me, young lady,' Luke said in an undertone.

Abby gave him a lopsided smile. 'Sorry about that. But hey, I thought you did a brilliant job. You seriously could have your own column.'

He gave her the side eye. 'Don't even think about it.'

Abby was thinking about lots of stuff. Like how warm and strong his arm felt around her waist. How the slightest movement of his fingers against hers sent an erotic charge right through her body and straight to her core. How when his eyes held hers something unravelled deep in her belly, like a ball of string let loose down a steep staircase.

And that kiss.

She hadn't stopped thinking about it. Her lips hadn't stopped tingling from it. How could a mouth that never smiled pack such a passionate punch? Her mouth would never be the same. It was permanently branded with the heat of Luke's kiss. Searing heat. Blistering heat. Heat that made her body shudder with excitement. She looked at his mouth and noticed a tiny smear from her shimmery lip-gloss was next to his top lip. She stepped up on tiptoe and lifted her hand and wiped it away. 'Oops, lip-gloss. All gone now.'

His eyes were as dark as sapphires, holding hers in a sensual lock as if he were mentally replaying every pulse-racing second of their kiss. His gaze went to her mouth, resting there for a thrumming beat before returning to her eyes. 'Did I tell you how beautiful you look tonight?'

'No, but—'

'You look dazzlingly beautiful,' Luke said. 'There isn't a man here who isn't wishing he could swap places with me right now.'

Abby knew he was only saying that because of the other guests close by. Of course, as her fiancé he would be expected to say nice things. Wonderful things. Things no one had ever told her before. He was acting a role and doing a damn fine job of it. But oh, how fabulous it would be if he really *did* mean them. When had anyone ever called her beautiful? She hadn't even been called pretty or becoming. She hadn't even been given the girl-next-door tag. She was bland. Unnoticeable. But how cool if he really thought her the most beautiful woman at the ball, just like Cinderella.

You are seriously out of your mind.

I know, I know. But he sounded so genuine.

'Thank you.' Abby smiled. 'But I'm not sure if I'll be able to eat anything while wearing this dress. My zip might not be able to take it.'

'Abby!' Felicity Kirby, her chief editor, came over in a cloud of exotic perfume and proceeded to air kiss Abby's cheeks. 'I'm literally gagging to meet your gorgeous Mr Perfect.' She beamed up at Luke and thrust out her hand. 'We would love to do an interview with you as soon as it can be arranged. Your work is absolutely amazing. I have a friend of a friend whose life was saved because of the tiny robotic surgical arm you designed for her brain surgery. I'll get one of my staff to contact you. Abby will give me your details and we'll—'

'I don't give interviews,' Luke said.

Felicity looked at him as if he'd just said he didn't breathe oxygen. 'But you must give an interview. Everyone wants to know about your romance with Abby. Like how on earth you kept your identity a secret for all this time. That in itself is worthy of a two-page spread. Now that we know who you are, we need to hear your side. You can do a guest blog with dating tips for the man about town. It'll be fabulous.'

'I'm sorry—I'm not interested.'

Felicity was undaunted and swung her gaze to Abby. 'Talk him into it, sweetie. He's a reader magnet. And so hot!' She fanned her face with her hand. 'No wonder you've been hiding him away for all this time. I wouldn't want to share him with anyone either.'

'I'll see what I can do.' Abby stretched her mouth into a smile.

Once Felicity had moved on, Luke pressed a firm warm hand in Abby's lower back, his low deep voice containing a thread of steel wrapped around every word. 'Do I have to say it again?'

'No. I heard you loud and clear.' Abby gave a little eye roll. 'No interviews.'

He let out a gusty sigh. 'I need a drink.'

She grabbed his hand and led him towards a drinks waiter carrying a tray. 'So do I.'

* * *

Luke stood with Abby a few minutes later with a glass of champagne in hand while she chatted to the other guests before the ballroom was opened for the main event. He put in a few words occasionally but he figured the less said the soonest mended. It was like being in a play but having read only half the script. Abby had told her readers things about 'him' that made him cringe. What sort of expert was he on romance? He had unwittingly sabotaged every relationship he'd ever been in and he had no intention of repeating those hard-learned mistakes.

And as for giving interviews. *Sheesh.* Were these people for real? If they wanted to interview him about his work then fine. But his private life was off limits. He could talk about work at a stretch, but he usually left it to his staff to handle media interviews. He liked working in the background and getting on with the research and design that led to the breakthroughs in medical robotic engineering that had changed lives all over the world. That was what he was an expert at doing. Not swanning around a gala ball making banal conversation with people he had nothing in common with and never would.

But it had to be said, Abby was looking smoking-hot tonight and he was quite enjoying the envious looks he was getting from the other men. He was also enjoying the way her body kept brushing up against his in the crowded foyer outside the ballroom. He kept his arm around her waist, and every now and again she would glance up and smile at him and something tightly closed in his chest would flick open.

He could still taste her.

The fruity sweet softness of her lips made him hungry for more. And, just like every other man present, he was having trouble keeping his eyes off her cleavage. Not that there wasn't lots of cleavage on show from the other women at the ball, but somehow it was Abby's that drew his eyes like a bee to highly prized pollen.

'Let's have a look at the silent auction while we wait,' Abby said, leading him to a display where various items were on show. 'You might find something you like.'

The only thing Luke liked so far was the way Abby looked in that dress. He was all for a bit of fundraising and it was an excellent cause, but none of the items in the silent auction particularly interested him, although there were a couple of original artworks that caught his eye. He had more than enough wealth to buy whatever he wanted when he wanted it. He was happy to make a donation without collecting any of the goods.

Abby seemed rather taken with one of the lucky door prizes that were also on show. She stood in front of the display of a week for two on a privately owned island in the Mediterranean with a wistful look on her face.

'Gosh, wouldn't this be great to win?' she said, pointing to the photo of a white sandy beach and the luxury villa that overlooked it. 'I'd love a week sunning myself on a private beach. Imagine being rich enough to own your own island!'

Luke had often thought about buying an island—somewhere to escape to and leave all the worries and pressures of life behind. Somewhere where the guilt that plagued him wouldn't follow. He'd even gone as far as looking at some online and taking a virtual tour. The thought of sand and surf and solitude was seriously tempting.

Almost as tempting as Abby.

'Great place for a honeymoon, eh, Abby?' one of the women from the magazine said on her way past.

Abby smiled at the woman and then turned back to Luke. 'You can win just by being here. How cool is that? There are stickers with numbers on them underneath all the chairs in the ballroom. The winning number will be announced at midnight.'

'Who would you take with you if you won?' Luke wasn't sure why he asked but she was looking so longingly at the display he couldn't stop himself in time.

She gave a self-deprecating laugh. 'I won't win. I've never won anything in my entire life.'

The doors to the ballroom were finally opened and Abby gasped when the stunning decorations came into view. She clutched Luke's hand in an excited can-you-believe-this? manner, reminding him of a small child at her first visit to a sweet shop. He had to admit the ballroom was nothing short of amazing. Garlands of fresh spring flowers adorned the room and taller arrangements were positioned

either side of the stage, where a live band was playing the welcome theme. The tables were laid with
crystal glasses and silver cutlery and there were even
more flowers as centrepieces as well as colourful he-
lium balloon trees.

The formal dinner began, and after Luke had exhausted his limited dinner party conversation reper-
toire he was relieved when the band started playing
just as the dessert course was being cleared away.
He took Abby's hand and stood. 'Would you like to
dance?'

Her smile was like a ray of sunshine on a bleak
winter's day. 'I'd love to.' She rose from her chair and
leaned close to his ear and whispered, 'By the way, I
told everyone you're an absolutely brilliant dancer.'

Of course you did. Luke mentally rolled his eyes.
'Let's hope I don't disappoint.'

Abby stepped on to the dance floor with Luke and
his arms brought her in close to his body. One of his
hands rested on her bare skin where the back of her
dress was scooped out low on her spine. Her skin
tingled and tightened and her breath all but stopped
when his pelvis came into contact with hers, the un-
mistakable stirring of his body making her heart
race as if she'd been running upstairs. Hundreds and
hundreds of stairs.

She had been right about him being a brilliant
dancer. His body moved in perfect sequence with
hers as if they had been training for a dancing com-
petition. Even the train on her dress wasn't an im-

pediment as he moved her around the dance floor without once stepping on it or allowing anyone else to either.

It had been so long since Abby had danced with anyone. Ever since she'd pretended to be in a relationship she hadn't been able to attend parties without finding a reasonable excuse for why her fiancé wasn't with her. It had been far easier not to go. She hadn't even been out to dinner for the last couple of years unless it was with a girlfriend. Her social life—meagre as it was—had ground to a halt. She'd been trying so hard to fit in, to appear normal, and just ended up feeling abnormal and missing out on all the things other people took for granted. Which was exactly like her childhood had been. Why did that keep happening to her?

Was she doomed to always be on the outside?

But now, with Luke's arms around her, she realised what she had been missing. It was fun to be out as a couple, to drink and eat together and dance to great music. It was even more fun knowing Luke and she had a secret of their own. That no one suspected they weren't the real deal. *Yay!* She had actually pulled it off. She wasn't going to be shamed and mocked and humiliated after all. But not only that, their conspiracy added a level of intimacy to their relationship that was strangely exciting. Titillating even. Everyone in the ballroom believed them to be madly in love.

Everyone thought they were lovers.

It would be kind of cool if you were the real deal.

Abby blinked away the thought. Why would she want to be *actually* engaged to Luke? He was only with her tonight under sufferance. He'd even set a strict time limit on it—two hours. *Two flipping hours!* Which proved he wasn't her type. He had zero spontaneity. He was stiff and formal and never smiled, and he didn't have a romantic bone in his body. He was a die-hard workaholic. He probably worked in his sleep. If he ever slept.

But that doesn't mean you couldn't be lovers for real.

As soon as the thought entered Abby's head it clung there like a lint ball on a mohair sweater. That kiss was the problem. Luke kissed like a man who knew his way around a woman's body. He had awakened something in *her* body, something that wasn't going to be a good doggy and lie down and go back to sleep.

Luke was currently single and had been for five years. She hadn't even had a lover and she could hardly take one while she was pretending to be engaged to Mr Perfect.

So why not Luke?

Abby wasn't a casual sex type of person, especially since her mother's approach to sex had been not just casual but contractual and chaotic. But how would she ever feel normal if she were still a virgin when she was thirty? Or forty? Ninety, even? But if she slept with Luke the problem would be solved. She could tick the box marked Normal. The more she thought about it, the more she was sold on the idea. It was an ideal solution.

All she had to do was convince Luke.

Luke guided her out of the way of an enthusiastic couple, bringing her even closer to his body. 'How soon can we leave?' he asked.

Abby leaned back to look up at him. 'Aren't you having a good time?'

He gave her a twisted movement of his lips that might have passed for a smile...well, if you were standing in the next county, maybe. 'Your time is almost up, Cinderella.'

Abby bit down on her lip and lowered her gaze to his perfectly aligned bow tie. Why did he have to remind her he had a stopwatch going on their evening? What did that say about her?

It said she was resistible, that was what it said.

Some smoking-hot seductress I turned out to be.

'What's wrong?' Luke said.

Abby brought her gaze back up to his and, taking a deep mental breath for courage, asked, 'Do you think we could kick on and have some supper somewhere after this?'

A small frown creased his forehead. 'Why?'

'Because I'm still hungry.'

'We just had a four-course dinner and you ate my dessert.'

Abby looked at his mouth, her stomach tilting when she thought of his kiss in the car. How could she survive on just one kiss? She was hungry for more of his kisses. She wanted to feast on them. To gorge on them. To go on a massive binge on them and she wouldn't even feel guilty in the morning. 'I'm not ready to go home yet. I haven't been out in ages and ages and…well, neither have you so it kind of makes sense to make the most of it.'

'Abby.'

She closed her eyes in a slow blink and sighed. 'Okay. Okay. I get it. Time's up and you want to go home and work. Forget I mentioned it.' She began to pull out of his hold to go back to their table but his fingers around her wrist stalled her.

He brought her back to stand in front of him, his hips brushing hers with such heart-stopping intimacy she had trouble remembering to breathe. His eyes were as dark as deep blue ink and framed by a frown that was thoughtful rather than his usual disapproving one. 'Don't you want to stick around for the lucky door prize draw?'

'I can barely win an argument let alone a prize like that.' *As our earlier conversation just confirmed.* 'Anyway, it's just supper together. That wouldn't be breaking any of your rules, would it?'

His eyes went to her mouth for a brief moment. Then he seemed to gather himself and he tucked her hand over his arm. 'Supper it is.'

Luke took Abby to an exclusive bar/supper club a few blocks from where the ball had been held. He'd been there a couple of times for work things and liked the atmosphere. They served coffee and cake as well as the regular cocktails and beverages.

Abby gave a cursory glance at the menu and sat back in the plush velvet-covered armchair. 'I'm going to have Sex on the Beach.'

He lifted one eyebrow and allowed his latent sense of dry humour to make a brief appearance. 'Still a bit cold for that, don't you think?'

Her cheeks developed tiny twin flags of colour. 'Have you ever done it on the beach?'

Luke had spent most of the night trying *not* to think about sex, especially sex with Abby. 'Couple of times.'

She leaned forward to rest her hands on her knees, her voice coming out as a whisper. 'Can I tell you a secret?'

He tried not to stare at her mouth, tried not to imagine it kissing its way down his body. Tried not to get hard, but hey, he was only human. 'Go for it.'

She blinked a couple of times and then ran the tip of her tongue over her lips, and he got a whole lot harder. Her gaze flicked away from his and the colour on her cheeks deepened. 'Never mind. Forget I said that. I think I've had too much champagne.'

Luke's interest was piqued by the way she seemed to be avoiding his gaze. What secret did she have? Was it something even more cringe-worthy she'd made up about their 'relationship'? 'What were you going to tell me?'

She pressed her lips together for a moment and then swallowed. 'I've… I've never done it.' Then she did a shocked wide-eyed thing and slapped both of her hands over her mouth as if she regretted her words. 'Ohmygofh.' Her hands pressing against her mouth muffled the words. 'I can't believe I just told you that.'

Luke had to mentally rewind to their previous conversation about outdoor sex. 'You mean you've never had sex on the beach?'

She lowered her hands from her mouth and avoided his gaze. 'Anywhere.'

Luke frowned. 'You mean anywhere outdoors?'

She glanced either side of her to see if anyone was sitting near enough to overhear and, leaning forward again, whispered, 'I've never had sex.'

He looked at her blankly for a moment, trying to get his head around what he'd heard, or thought he'd heard. 'Let me get this straight... You're saying you've *never* slept with anyone? Is that what you're saying?'

She rolled her lips back inside her mouth and gave a single nod.

He leaned forward to make sure he wasn't mishearing her. 'You're a virgin?'

'Yup.'

Luke sat back as if someone had shoved him with the end of a telegraph pole. 'You're joking, right?'

Abby shook her head. 'Nope.'

She was a virgin? Abby Hart, the relationships and dating expert was a virgin? Why the hell hadn't she been intimate with anyone? She was twenty-three years old. Most modern girls lost their virginity well before then, unless they had religious reasons for being celibate.

'But why?' Luke asked, genuinely confused.

She shrugged and looked at the bowl of salted peanuts on the table between their knees. She took a peanut and popped it into her mouth and chewed and swallowed. She reached for another and another and did the same. 'Did you know it's virtually impossible to eat only one peanut? I've done extensive research on this. It literally cannot be done. Try it.'

Luke moved the peanuts out of her reach. 'Abby, look at me.'

She slowly brought her gaze back to his. Her tongue swept salt crumbs off her lips and he suppressed a groan. He couldn't stop thinking about her tongue doing that to him. 'I know it's a little weird, but I never really felt emotionally ready... I mean, before now.'

His heart slammed against his chest wall. 'Before...*now?*'

She tucked a loose strand of hair behind her ear and eyed the peanuts like a puppy looked at an out of reach treat. 'I sort of wanted to a couple of times, but I always put a stop to things out of fear I would make a fool of myself or...or something.' Her gaze met his. 'Anyway, I figure if we have sex anything like we dance then I think we'd be good together in bed.'

'That's another theory of yours, is it?'

'Yes, well, of course it's a theory because I haven't put it to the test yet, but that's the whole point of this conversation.' She gave him a smile that looked a little shaky around the edges. 'So, what do you say? Will you do it?'

Luke was having trouble getting his brain into gear. Other parts of his anatomy were well on their way, but his brain? No. Sleeping with Abby was the sort of trouble he could do without. Apart from the fact she was his kid sister's best friend, Abby was trouble, period. She wanted things he didn't want.

You want her.

He did. Badly. So badly he could feel the lust throbbing right here and now in his loins. Lust like he had never felt before. Not even as a horny hormonal teenager.

But it didn't mean he was going to have her.

He didn't get involved with virgins. Abby was the poster girl for the white knight and white wedding and white picket fence package. Everything she wrote in her column was about being in a secure and happy relationship.

Nothing he could offer her was anything near secure.

He didn't do commitment.

Luke leaned forward to take her hands in his to get her full attention. 'Listen to me, Abby—'

'We don't have to tell Ella,' she said. 'She doesn't even know I'm a virgin.'

He did a rapid blink. 'She doesn't? But I thought you two were best friends?'

She lowered her gaze to their joined hands. 'We are but we've only known each other for the last four years. There are some things you don't even tell your best friend.'

Luke could relate to that. There were things he

hadn't told a soul. Nor ever would. There was no point because talking about it would never take away his guilt. How could it? He gave her hands a little squeeze to get her to look at him again. 'Why didn't you feel you could tell her?'

A screen came down on her face and she pulled her hands away. 'Look, if you don't want to do it then let's leave it at that. I'll find someone else. Eventually.'

Luke's gut clenched. Which someone else? Some stranger she picked up in a bar? Or on a dating app? And why was she acting so closed-off all of a sudden? How well did his sister know Abby Hart? Did anyone really know her? Why had she got to the age of twenty-three without doing the deed? She was attractive and sexy and funny. She surely wouldn't have been short on offers?

Damn it, if he wasn't careful he'd be offering himself.

The waiter came to take their order and Luke was relieved when Abby ordered a simple cup of tea instead of the cocktail. A part of him was glad she wasn't having the sex-inspired cocktail but another part felt a twinge of disappointment he couldn't explain—didn't want to.

He waited until the waiter left to get their drinks before he spoke. 'I think you should think carefully before you pick up someone to sleep with either in a bar or online. There are some real creeps out there who might not be as nice as they seem on the surface.'

'Save your big brother lecture for your sister,'

Abby said and scooped up a handful of peanuts. 'I can take care of myself.'

Luke wished he felt more of a big brother to her than what he was feeling right now. He hadn't felt this degree of lust in years. It was as if it was taking over his body, his brain. His self-control. He couldn't stop thinking about her invitation. What exactly did she want from him?

Don't ask.

It was better not to know so he wasn't tempted beyond his endurance. Hell, he *was* already tempted beyond his endurance. His endurance better get back into shape quick smart or he was going to be in big trouble.

'You sure you don't want something to eat with your cup of tea?' Luke asked after the waiter delivered their drinks.

'I'm not hungry now.' She dusted the salt from her fingers. 'I've eaten too many peanuts.'

Luke had his own theory. Abby was exactly like eating a peanut. Making love to her once would never be enough.

Nowhere near enough.

Her phone made a pinging sound from inside her evening purse. She leaned forward to take it out and her gaze widened to the size of the saucer under her teacup. 'Oh, my God...'

'What's wrong? Is it bad news?'

She looked up from the phone and smiled. 'Guess what? You won the island holiday lucky door prize.'

CHAPTER FOUR

ABBY COULDN'T BELIEVE IT. Luke had won the prize *she* had been drooling over. How unfair was that? He could afford to pay for his own holiday. He could probably afford his own flipping island. Why had she sat in the unlucky seat instead of his winning one?

No doubt this was the universe's way of rubbing in her disappointment after Luke declined her offer of a fling. How could she not be feeling a little disappointed he'd rejected her offer? Had she made a mistake by telling him she was still a virgin? She still wasn't sure why she had told him—it had sort of slipped out in an unguarded moment. The combination of the magic of the evening in his company and all that champagne she'd drunk at the ball had loosened her tongue as if it was greased.

What had she been thinking?

She hadn't been thinking. She'd been feeling. Feeling things she had never felt before. Wicked things, like how exciting it would be to be Luke's lover. To enjoy more of those steaming-hot kisses and much more besides. Like having his hands ca-

ress every inch of her body, to have him possess her
and take her to the heights of human pleasure—the
sort of pleasure she had only ever experienced alone
and never felt truly satisfied by.

Making love with Luke would be more than satis-
fying. How could it not be? His kiss had awakened a
need in her body, a need that even now clamoured for
attention. It was like he had set a primal beat thrumming in her flesh that only his touch could assuage.

Abby turned her phone around so Luke could see
the message Felicity, her chief editor, had sent. 'See?
Your seat number was the lucky one. They sent the
message to me as they didn't have your contact details.'

He leaned forward to read the text. 'Can they re-
draw it?'

Abby frowned. 'You mean you don't want it?'

His expression was so difficult to read, hiero-
glyphics would have been easier. 'Clearly not as
much as you did.'

Abby looked at the message again, vainly hoping they'd got the seat numbers wrong. But no, there
it was in black and white. 'There's a time limit on
the offer. You have to go within the next month.'
She looked back at him to see him frowning at her.
'What?'

'Is it transferable?'

'Transferable?'

'Can I gift it to you instead of taking it myself?'
Luke asked.

It was a nice gesture but how could she go alone?

Who went to a private island for a holiday on their own? How normal was that? It would make her feel even more of a pariah. Anyway, people from work would expect her to go with Luke and blog about the holiday and post pictures. It would seem odd if she didn't. And what would everyone say if she took a girlfriend instead of her fiancé? Luke had made it clear he wasn't interested in a fling so she was certain he wouldn't want to go with her.

She was facing the same dilemma all over again. If she went on the holiday on her own it would be like turning up to the ball on her own.

She would be outed as a big fat *abnormal* fraud.

Abby shoulders slumped. 'That's sweet of you, Luke, but even if it was transferable I won't be able to go.'

'Why not?'

She put the phone back in her purse with another sigh. 'I'd have to use it within the next month.'

'Why is that a problem?' Two horizontal pleats formed between his eyes. 'Can't you take some time off from work?'

'Taking leave isn't the problem,' Abby said. 'I have plenty of time owed me. It's taking someone with me that's the kicker.'

Something passed over his retinas like ripples on the surface of a lake. Then he frowned again, deeper this time. 'Stop that thought right there.'

Abby put on her most beguiling expression. 'What thought?'

'I'm not going with you on that damn holiday,

Abby. I told you the deal. Tonight for two hours—and we're over time as it is.'

'But it's only for a week,' she said. 'And I've always wanted to stay on a private island—any island, actually. I haven't had a proper holiday for ages and it would be so cool to stay in a luxury villa and—'

'Take a girlfriend,' he said. 'Take Ella.'

'Ella won't go during school term, she's way too dedicated a teacher to do something like that,' Abby said. 'And anyway, I can't take a friend. Everyone will be expecting me to go with you, especially since you won the prize. How will I explain it if you don't go with me?'

'Put that creative imagination of yours to use and think of something.' His sarcasm cut like a hunting knife.

'Are you only saying no because of what I told you?'

'I'm saying no because you and I getting it on is a crazy idea.'

'Why is it crazy?' Abby was trying to keep her ego from curling up in the foetal position and rocking in the corner. Was she so disgusting—so abnormal—that he couldn't bear the thought of making love to her? Had she misread his kiss and his touch? His arousal?

'Abby...' His breath came out in a long whoosh as if he was trying to keep control and was only just managing to do so. 'I'm not denying I find you attractive. I do. But that doesn't mean I'm going to act on it.'

'But why not?' Abby was hoping she might win this argument as compensation for not winning the holiday. 'Why is my being a virgin such a big issue for you? I have to have sex some time. It might as well be with you—someone I know personally instead of a complete stranger.'

'You and me? That's crazy talk.' His voice had a gravelly intensity to it, as if he was digging deep to hold on to his resolve. 'You want marriage and all it entails. I'm not interested in going down that path, with you or anyone.'

'Is that because of your parents' divorce?' Abby said. 'Ella told me how awful it was.'

Luke's mouth thinned as if he had just eaten something bitter as bile. 'Yeah, well, it doesn't get much worse than when your dad suddenly announces he has a mistress and a baby on the way the night before your fifteenth birthday. But it's not because of that. I don't want the complication of a long-term relationship.'

'Where did you get the idea I'm asking for anything long-term from you?' Abby said. 'I just don't want to be a virgin any more. I feel embarrassed about it. Really embarrassed. That's why I haven't said anything to Ella. I feel like a freak for not having had sex yet.'

'I'm sorry but I can't help you with that.' He picked up his coffee and drained the contents, placing the cup back down with a definitive clunk.

Abby crossed her legs and folded her arms, her

lips pushed forward in a moue. 'Excuse me while I do some urgent CPR on my bludgeoned ego.'

A flicker of concern went through his gaze. 'It's not meant as an insult. Think about it. How would we explain it to Ella?'

'I think she would be thrilled you were finally taking a break from work.'

His features reminded her of a shuttered window. 'I run a global company. There isn't time for—'

'No wonder you get migraines,' Abby cut in. 'You push yourself too hard. I have a theory about people who are workaholics. They fill their days with work because they don't want to face what's missing in their life.'

'Yeah? Well, I have a little theory too.' His eyes were like laser pointers at a forensics lecture. 'People who pretend to be someone they're not do it because they're afraid people won't like the real version of them.' He rose from the chair and scooped up his jacket from where he'd left it. 'Come on. It's time to go.'

Abby remained silent on the drive back to her flat. Not that Luke addressed any comments to her. He was as taciturn as usual. What right did he have to analyse her? He didn't know squat about her. He didn't know how hard it had been for her growing up. How embarrassing it was to have grown up in foster homes, never knowing when you were going to be moved on to another family, another school, and trying to make friends with people who already had enough friends.

Her life had been one long struggle to fit in.

To be normal.

Luke might be a little screwed-up about his parents' divorce but at least his dad hadn't tried to kill someone. His mother hadn't slept with men for money while her little daughter was nearby. His mother hadn't then died of an overdose and left him in the deadlocked flat until someone found him the following day.

That was Abby's life story. The script she couldn't change, no matter how hard she tried. She was always being left to fend for herself.

What right did Luke have to criticise her? She liked who she was. She was a good person. She had friends, a job and a roof over her head.

But when Luke turned the corner into Abby's street she had to rethink the roof over her head bit. There were gas technician vans and two police cars with lights flashing and an ambulance outside her block of flats as well as a circle of nosy onlookers being ushered back by the police. 'Oh, my God, w-what's going on?' Her voice shook with shock.

Luke wound down his window when a police officer came over. 'What's happening?'

'There's been a major gas leak,' the officer said. 'The building's been evacuated until further notice. That section of the road is closed.' He pointed to a detour sign. 'You'll have to take a right over here.'

'But I live in that building!' Abby leaned across Luke to speak to the police officer.

'You can't go home until the problem's been

sorted,' the officer said so firmly it sounded like it had been underlined.

'How long will it take?' Abby asked.

The officer gave a shrug. 'There's been no announcement made as yet. You'll have to check the gas company's website for an update.'

'But I need to get some clothes and stuff.'

'Sorry. The area is cordoned off until further notice.'

Abby sat back in her seat with a slump of her shoulders. 'Great. Now I'm homeless. Go me.'

Luke wound up the window and drove to the detour. 'I'll book you into a hotel. You can stay there until things are back to normal.'

'I can't afford a hotel,' Abby said. 'And I absolutely refuse your offer to pay for it if that's what you're thinking.'

He pulled the car over to a parking bay further along the street they were on and turned to look at her. 'What about calling Ella? She might be able to put you up for a few days.'

Abby gnawed at her lip. 'I can't stay with her. It's too far to travel for work.'

'What about your family? Don't they live somewhere in London?'

Abby looked out of the window. It was at times like this that it hit her all over again how different her life was from everyone else's. She had no bolthole. No safe harbour to bunk down until a crisis was over.

She was totally alone.

'I can't stay with them. Their house is too small.'

Abby sensed rather than saw his frown. 'But I thought you told Ella they live in a big mansion in—?'

She sent him a sideways look. 'I lied, okay? They live in a council flat in Birmingham.'

'Why'd you lie about that?'

'Because…because they're not even my family…' Abby blew out a sigh. 'They're my foster family.'

There was a silence, broken by the rumbling of the car's idling engine.

'Your foster family?' Luke's voice was a mixture of concern and surprise. 'Where are your parents?'

She gave him a weary look. 'Believe me, you don't want to know.'

His frown was so deep his eyebrows made a black bridge over his eyes. 'How long did you live with a foster family?'

'The last one for six and a half years, and that was the longest I stayed anywhere,' Abby said. 'The ones before that, four and two years respectively, and the ones before that a few months at a time… I've been in the foster care system since I was five.' She didn't mention the six months she'd spent living with her father before she was taken into permanent care.

She preferred *not* to think about that.

Luke sat on an angle in his seat, looking at her as if he had never seen her before. But then in a way he hadn't. Abby had made sure no one in her present life knew anything of her past life. But now she had told him she felt a strange sense of lightness, as if something heavy she'd been carting around had slightly eased its load.

'Have you told Ella about this?' he asked.

Abby shook her head. 'I've thought about it… many times. But in the end I didn't see the point. It's not as if she's ever going to meet any of them.'

'She would be hurt to think you kept this from her.'

'I know… But you know how she worries over everyone. I didn't want her fussing over me, trying to compensate me for my crappy childhood. I just want to be like everyone else. Normal.'

'Whatever the hell that is.' His tone was wry.

There was another silence.

Luke started drumming his fingers on the steering wheel as if he was deep in thought, his gaze focused on the drizzle of rain sliding down the windscreen. He turned back to look at her at the same time he put the car back into gear. 'You can stay with me until your flat is ready.'

Abby looked at him in surprise. 'You wouldn't mind?'

Something at the back of his eyes indicated he minded a great deal but his voice was reassuring. 'It'll be fine. I'm hardly there in any case, other than to sleep.'

'It's very kind of you, Luke. Hopefully it'll only be for a couple of days. I promise not to disturb you too much.'

He gave a soft grunt as if the notion of her disturbing him was a given. 'But—just to be clear—you'll be sleeping in the spare room.'

* * *

A short time later, Luke unlocked his front door and followed Abby inside. Having her come and stay with him was a way to get to know her a bit more. To uncover more of the secrets she had kept about her background. Or so he told himself. He knew it was dangerous inviting her to sleep at his house. Sharing any personal space with her was dangerous. His house was large but it would need to be twice the size of Buckingham Palace for him to feel safe from the temptation she presented.

The stuff she'd told him about her background had shocked him. Why had she kept it a secret even from his sister, Ella? Who were Abby's biological parents and why had she been taken away from them so young? Had she been abused? Neglected? The thought of it was sickening. Was that why she was so determined to get to the ball tonight, to raise funds for underprivileged children? No wonder she couldn't bear not to go. He felt a heel now for making such an issue out of going with her.

Abby's past and the lengths she'd gone to keep it secret reminded him of the way he kept stuff to himself. He couldn't blame her for being a little hesitant to tell people things they might judge her for. People made judgements all the time on who your parents were, where you went to school, your accent, your income, the car you drove and where you lived. Even who your friends were.

Luke could understand now why she had been so taken with that luxury holiday. It was sad to think she had probably never been on a proper holiday with her parents. At least he had enjoyed some happy times with his family before his father dropped his bombshell the day before Luke's fifteenth birthday. Holidays after his parents' divorce had been pretty miserable. His mother would spend most of it crying or staring at couples walking hand in hand with a wistful look on her face. Ella, being nine years younger than him, had latched on to him in the absence of the father she'd adored and who no longer had any time for her, which meant Luke hadn't been free to do the things other teenagers his age did.

Luke closed the front door and looked at Abby's downcast expression. Her shoulders were slumped and some tendrils of her hair had fallen down around her heart-shaped face. It had been a big night for her, capped off by coming home to find her flat uninhabitable. A sudden wave of empathy swept through him and he had to stop himself from pulling her into a hug in case he was tempted to not let her go.

'Tired?' he said.

'Exhausted—but I can't help thinking what am I going to do about my clothes?'

Luke would be quite happy if she didn't wear any. Ever again. But that was a dangerous thought he shouldn't be allowing inside his head. 'We can sort that out tomorrow. Maybe they'll let you back in to fetch a few things even if they don't allow you to move back in.'

'What about Kimberley's clothes? Maybe I could—'

'You're a different size.'

A flicker of something passed through her gaze. 'Ella showed me a photo of her once. Kimberley was really beautiful and slim, wasn't she?'

'I didn't mean it that way.' Luke mentally rolled his eyes. What was it with women and their weight? Abby had a beautiful body—a gorgeous, luscious body he was having trouble keeping his hands off. Sure, her body wasn't stick-thin but he had always been annoyed by his ex's obsession with being reed-slim. It had been one of the reasons he'd ended their relationship. One of the many reasons. He couldn't face another meal out with Kimberley moving the food around her plate without eating a morsel. He'd found it cute how Abby had eaten his dessert tonight as well as her own.

'I only have a couple of her things anyway,' he said. 'I've been meaning to give them to her family but never seem to get around to doing it.'

Abby gave him a thoughtful look 'Do you think it's because you're not ready to finally let go?'

Luke moved past her, undoing his bow tie as he went. 'I'll get you a toothbrush and show you which bathroom to use. Follow me.'

Abby followed him upstairs, where he opened the door to one of the spare rooms. It had a bathroom just down the corridor but she couldn't help noticing it was the furthest bedroom from his. It was another slap down to her ego. Did he think she'd come crawling into his bed during the night and try and seduce him? Clearly she had some work to do in the seduction stakes. A lot of work.

'Do you want something to sleep in? A shirt or something?' he asked.

'Don't worry. I can sleep in my... Actually, I'm not wearing any underwear. I didn't want any panty lines under my dress.'

Argh! Why did you tell him that?

His gaze flicked over her as if he were imagining her naked under her ball gown. But then he gave a rapid blink as if he was clearing his mental vision. 'Right, well, then. I'll leave you to get settled. Goodnight.'

Abby closed the door once he'd left and leant back against it with a sigh. Did he have to make it any clearer he didn't want her? Most men would have jumped at the chance for a bit of no-strings sex.

What was wrong with her?

Was she so hideous Luke couldn't stomach the thought of being intimate with her?

Or was it more about him than her? Was he still so hung up on the loss of his girlfriend he couldn't bear the thought of making love with someone else?

But he'd said he hadn't been in love with Kimberley. Why then would he remain celibate for so long?

Why was he still punishing himself?

CHAPTER FIVE

ABBY WAS SO tired she barely made it to the bed before her eyes closed. But during the night she woke with a start, wondering at first where she was. One of the legacies of her crazy childhood was a tendency to be a light sleeper. And all those years of sleeping at different foster homes made her jumpy whenever she woke in unfamiliar surroundings. She woke at the slightest sound, her heart racing, her legs feeling fizzy as the fight or flight reflex switched on.

She felt the mattress enveloping her like a hug and she breathed out a deep sigh of relaxation. At least it was the weekend tomorrow so she didn't have to front up to work still dressed in her ball gown.

But then she heard the sound again.

She sat upright, cocking her head to try and identify the noise. Was she imagining things? Had it been a dream?

Abby lay back down, remonstrating with herself for being so pathetic. Luke's house had top-notch security. Her fears of a masked intruder sneaking into her room were as likely as Luke himself coming in and saying he'd changed his mind about sleeping with her.

Not going to happen.

She closed her eyes again and tried to go back to sleep but her body felt twitchy and restless. And she was so thirsty her mouth felt like she'd been sucking on a stale gym sock. She threw off the covers and wrapped her naked body in the fluffy bath sheet towel she'd used earlier.

Abby tiptoed down the corridor but then she noticed a thin strip of light shining underneath Luke's bedroom door. She paused by the door, tilting her head against it to listen. She heard a groan and then the sound of something being knocked over and hitting the floor with a muted thud. 'Luke?' She rapped her knuckles gently against the door. 'Are you okay?'

There was the sound of a muttered curse and then footsteps padding across the carpet towards the door. The door opened and Luke looked down at her through squinted eyes, his features pinched and a ghastly shade of grey. He was wearing a pair of long grey cotton pyjama bottoms that were riding low on his trim hips. And, in spite of how unwell he looked, Abby had never seen anything so sexy.

'I'm fine.' His voice was in his gruff bear mode. 'Go back to bed.'

'You are so not fine,' Abby said, seeing the spasm of pain in his gaze. 'You look terrible.' How had she thought he was drunk six months ago? It was obvious he was unwell both then and now. She felt thoroughly ashamed. She had jumped to conclusions and misjudged him.

He leaned his forehead on the edge of the door as if he didn't have the strength to keep it upright on his neck. 'It's just a headache. It'll pass once the medication kicks in.'

Abby wasn't a sufferer of migraines but she'd read enough about them to know they could be crippling. Sufferers couldn't bear light or the slightest sound, and finding a quiet dark place until the migraine passed was usually the best solution. She took Luke's hand and ignoring his weak protest, led him back to the bed. 'Lie down,' she said in a soft voice. 'I'll get you a damp face cloth.'

Surprisingly, he did as she said and lay on his back on the bed, his long legs stretched out, his feet splayed outwards. Abby left him lying there while she went to his en suite bathroom and rinsed a face-cloth under the cold water tap. She squeezed it out and came back to him and, perching on the edge of the bed, laid the cool cloth gently across his clammy forehead. He made a low sound of appreciation but his eyes stayed closed.

After a while, Abby realised he was drifting in and out of sleep, his body twitching and his closed eyelids flickering as if trying to combat pulses of searing pain. She stayed beside him, reluctant to leave him until she was sure he was resting peacefully.

Her eyes started to flicker, not from pain but tiredness. She was still dressed in nothing but a bath sheet and, while it covered her adequately, she longed to slip between the sheets and close her heavy-as-dumb-bells eyelids.

Just for a few minutes.

Once the thought was inside her head it was impossible to resist the lure of the comfortable bed. It was a king-sized one, surely big enough for him not to even notice her there. Or maybe it was an emperor-sized one. Did such a thing exist? It was certainly big enough for a football team, plus some spectators.

He wouldn't even know she had been here.

She carefully peeled back the covers and slipped in, well away from Luke's sleeping form. Her head went down on the feather pillow and everything that was tense and tired inside her body began to slowly relax, as if she was a tightly wound ball of wool and someone was starting to unravel her.

Luke made a soft noise and rolled over to his side, facing away from her. Abby held her breath, her heart hammering until she was certain he was soundly asleep, and then she finally closed her eyes and the ball of wool in her tense muscles slowly and blissfully unwound the rest of the way...

Abby woke to find one of Luke's strong arms across her body and his legs brushing up against hers from behind. Slats of bright sunshine stole through the gap in the curtains, indicating it was well past dawn. What time was it? How long had she been sleeping?

Eek! She was sleeping in Luke's bed!

She suddenly realised she was naked and, even

though she moved a foot experimentally to search for it, there was no sign of the bath sheet she had wrapped around herself the night before.

How had she ended up naked in his bed with her limbs tangled with his?

Had they fooled around? Had she made a sleepy pass at him? Surely if they had made love she would remember it? She would most definitely remember it. She might occasionally forget to buy milk or bread or to pay the minimum payment on her credit card but she would never forget making love with Luke.

Abby closed her eyes again and tried to recall anything from the time after she'd slipped in beside him. Nope. Nothing but a blank…although there was that delicious little dream where someone had kissed the back of her shoulder. A prickly, stubbly sort of kiss followed by a lazy lion-like lick of the tongue that had sent a shiver over her skin.

Right now the back of her neck was being tickled by Luke's rhythmic breathing, and she could feel the rise and fall of his chest between her shoulder blades. She stayed perfectly still, not wanting to disturb him, mainly because she was sure he would spring away if he knew what he was doing.

How nice was this? How cosy and sexy and slightly wicked. She liked the feeling of being held, of being spooned as if she was treasured, special. She lay there quietly registering all the sensory hot spots on her body where it was touching his. The differences between their bodies, his hard-muscled frame and her softer one, made her feel womanly and feminine in a way she never had felt before. Even the scent of their bodies was different, but the thought of those intimate smells mingling with each other was strangely, excitingly arousing.

Luke made a sleepy sound that was part murmur, part groan and gathered her even closer, his face nuzzling into the side of her neck, the graze of his morning stubble making her skin shiver like a filly trying to shake off a fly.

Abby closed her eyes, feigning sleep, trying to get her breathing as rhythmic as his, which wasn't easy given her heart was stuttering like an old tractor engine.

One of his legs came over the top of hers and he pulled her against his morning erection. Abby had never felt anything so erotic and exciting in her life. Her girly bits clapped their hands in glee and her breasts tingled from the soft prickle of his masculine hair where his strong forearm was resting just below them.

'Mmm...' Luke's voice was a sexy hum against her neck that made her nerves fizz and flicker.

Abby was wondering how far she could push her luck when he suddenly jerked away from her with an expletive. 'What the freaking hell?'

She turned over to see him staring at her in abject horror. *So much for her self-esteem. Off to the corner with you to suck your thumb and rock.*

'What did I do?' Luke asked in a tone she hadn't heard him use before. It was strangled and hoarse as if he had swallowed a pineapple. 'Did we—? Tell me we—I didn't—'

'Nothing happened, Luke,' Abby said, letting out a frustrated sigh. 'I think we just somehow gravitated together while we were sleeping.'

He threw off the covers and stood up by the side of the bed, his expression dark and frowning. 'Why are you sleeping...*naked* in my bed?' His stress over the word 'naked' was like a skewer through the balloon-thin skin of her self-esteem.

Abby pulled the bed sheet over her body and sat up. 'I was worried about you. I didn't want to leave you until I was certain you were asleep. But somehow I—'

'Thought you'd whip off your clothes and jump into bed with me?' His tone couldn't have been more scathing than if he was reprimanding a rebellious teenager. 'For God's sake, Abby. I could have—' He scraped his hair back off his forehead, his mouth snapping closed as if he couldn't bear to say out loud what he could have done.

'I was wearing a towel—a big one—but it must have slipped off.' Abby glanced at the foot of the bed and saw a lump under the covers. 'There it is. See? It must have got pushed down there when we—'

'When we *what*?' His voice cracked like an egg on concrete. 'Damn it, Abby, I could have hurt you.'

'You didn't do anything I didn't want,' Abby said. 'I liked being spooned. No one's ever done that to me before. I liked the feel of your body behind mine. It was—'

'Stop.' He held his hand up as if he was stopping traffic. 'Stop it right there. This is not happening.'

'It is happening, Luke.' She clutched the sheet around her breasts to keep it secure. 'You want me.'

'It's a reflex,' he said. 'It happens to every man in the morning. It means nothing.'

Abby decided it was time to test a little theory of hers. She swung her legs off the bed and stood up and let the sheet slip so more than half of her breasts were showing. His eyes ran over her cleavage and the upper swell of her breasts, his throat bobbing up and down over a swallow.

'I'll just be going then.' She moved past him to leave the room but his hand reached for her and came down on her forearm. She stopped and turned to face him, her arm buzzing with sensation where his fingers lay. 'Am I really so unappealing to you?'

He frowned. 'God, no. I want you but—'

'Then why not have me?' Abby moved closer. 'I want you.'

His hand fell away from her arm. 'You want more than I can give.'

'I'm asking you to sleep with me, not marry me and have your babies. Why is having a fling with me so unthinkable to you?'

'I don't want what happens between us to get in the way of your relationship with my sister,' he said. 'Or for that matter for my relationship with her to be damaged.'

'It won't be,' Abby said. 'Ella knows you went to the ball with me. She's probably seen the photos of us last night all over social media. She'll be happy for you that you've moved on and she'll be happy for me as long as I'm happy.'

'And how long will your happiness last?' he said. 'I know how this works. The longer two people have sex together, especially if the sex is good, the harder it is to let go. Particularly for women.' Something about his expression made Abby wonder if there was more to that last comment than there appeared at face value.

'What if we were to set a time limit on it then?' Abby said. 'We could draw up an agreement so we both agree on the terms.'

His mouth opened and closed as if he were going to say something but changed his mind. Then he let out an exasperated sigh. 'Will you please get dressed? I can't think straight with you standing there like that.'

Abby stroked her hand down the length of his chest, stopping just above the waistline of his tented pyjama pants. 'Do you really want me to get dressed?' She channelled her inner sexy siren with a whisper-soft voice.

He swallowed again and took her by the hips almost roughly. 'No, damn it, I don't.' He brought his mouth down to hers in a blistering kiss that shot a bolt of lightning through her flesh.

She pressed closer, her barely covered breasts crushed against his chest, his sprinkling of hair intensifying the sensation like all her nerves were on the outside of her skin. The sheet was slipping but she didn't care. She was too caught up in the moment. The thrilling moment of feeling Luke's flaming lust. *For her.* His erection jutted against her as if his body was taking control, going on impulse not reason. His tongue came in search of hers in a smooth sexy slide and another hot spurt of longing darted through her.

He groaned against her mouth, a groan that sounded as if it had come from deep inside him. Somewhere deep and dark and closed off but now finally creaking open. His hands moved from grasping her hips to mould her to his body, one arm a steel band around her back, the other gliding up the back of her neck to splay his fingers into her hair, making her scalp tingle as if sherbet was trickling through her hair.

But just as suddenly as the kiss started, it was over.

Luke pulled back from her and released her, his expression a contorted mixture of lust and disgust. 'That should never have happened. I'm sorry.'

Abby wasn't one bit sorry. Her lips were buzzing, her inner core was fizzing and every cell in her body was clapping their hands for an encore. But there was only so much rejection her self-esteem could take. Was the disgust she'd seen on his face for him or for her?

She had offered herself and he had said an emphatic *no*. His body might want her but the rational part of him didn't.

Both parts of her wanted him. Every part.

Every throbbing, aching part.

Abby gathered the sheet more securely around her body, avoiding his gaze. 'I'm going to have a shower. I guess I'll see you downstairs.'

'I have to go in to work for most of today.'

'Do you usually work on Saturdays? No, don't answer that. I already know. Of course you do because you have no life other than work,' she said in a teasing tone, desperately wanting him to see how damaging it was to deny himself any longer.

'I took you to the ball as agreed, okay?'

'Which you enjoyed.' Abby eyeballed him. 'Didn't you? Go on, admit it, Luke. You had a good time.'

His gave an indifferent shrug. 'The ball was important to you so I took you. End of story.'

'What about that kiss?'

Something flickered over his features like a glitch in a film reel. 'What about it?'

'Actually, there were two,' Abby said. 'The one last night in the car and this one just now. You seemed to enjoy those too.'

He did something with his mouth, a sort of twitch and sideways movement of his lips, as if to remove the memory of those kisses. But his gaze was as shuttered as a beach house in winter. 'I'll be back around six this evening.' He took a couple of strides for the en suite bathroom.

'Aren't you forgetting something?'

He turned and frowned. 'What?'

She pointed to the sheet she was wrapped in. 'I don't have any clothes.'

'What about the dress you wore last night?'

Abby rolled her eyes like the ball bearings in a child's puzzle maze. 'Duh. That would be akin to the walk of shame to be seen out in public in a ball gown in broad daylight. Very morning-after-the-night before-ish. I hate feeling so…so vulnerable. So exposed.'

He seemed to be having some trouble getting his voice to work. He kept opening and closing his mouth as if he were having some sort of internal debate. 'Right, then I'll show you Kimberley's things and maybe there'll be something you could make do with until you go home.'

But when Luke pulled back the sliding door of his wall-to-wall wardrobe there were only a few female items hanging to one side, well away from his neatly ordered shirts and ties and crisply seamed trousers.

'Help yourself,' he said, stepping away as if even looking at the clothes was painful.

Abby worked her way through the half dozen or so coat hangers but it felt a little creepy to be handling a dead woman's clothes. They were beautifully made and she didn't have to peep at any of the labels to know they were all from high street designers. What must Luke think of *her* jumble sale assortment compared to these gorgeous things?

She sighed and stepped away from the wardrobe. 'I'm sorry but I don't think I can wear any of those.' She turned to face him. 'Why do you keep them there? Why not put them in another cupboard, or pack them up in a box or something?'

Luke slid the door back across, his expression as closed as the door. 'I haven't had time.'

'You've had five years, surely that's long enough to—?'

'I'll get to it eventually.'

'Like when you're moving into a retirement home?' Abby said. 'It's not healthy to keep that stuff for so long. It'll hold you back from—'

'I hardly think you're the one who should be lecturing me on how to live my life.'

Abby recognised his shot over the bow for what it was. A defence mechanism. She backed down. 'I'm sorry for prying, Luke. It's none of my business why you've still got those clothes there. And you're absolutely right. I have no right to be criticising you on how you live your life when mine is such a shambles.'

He drew in a breath and then let it out in a staggered stream. 'I keep them there to remind me.'

'Of…of her? Kimberley?'

He moved to the other side of the room to stare out of the window, his back turned towards her.

The silence was as intense as an unexpected music interval…the audience poised, waiting, waiting, waiting for the next note to be struck.

Abby wanted to prompt him, to encourage him to share whatever he was holding back, but she knew it would be better for him to be the one who broke the silence.

'Kimberley died the night I ended my relationship with her.'

Abby's heart gave a painful spasm and her breath caught on a thorn in her throat. 'Oh, no... I'm so sorry...'

He turned to face her, his expression a picture of regret and self-recrimination. 'I've thought about that night thousands of times, wondering if I'd said things differently, waited another day or two, a week even to call things off between us, if she would still be alive.'

Abby stared at him in shock. 'You feel...*responsible* for her death? But—'

His gaze was suddenly direct. 'Wouldn't you?'

She would. She very definitely would. Didn't she still blame herself for her mother's death? She still blamed herself for not being able to unlock the front door of the flat in time for help to be summoned for her mother, despite only being a child. 'Luke... I think it's perfectly understandable you would feel that way. I'm so sorry you've been carrying that guilt for so long. It must be unbearable.'

There was a slight relaxation of the muscles on his face as if her sympathetic words had eased some of his inner tension. 'It never goes away. The guilt of how I handled the breakup. How I handled the whole relationship, when it comes to that.'

'Were you ever happy with her?'

'Not particularly.' He let out a rusty-sounding sigh. 'We met when I was dealing with yet another one of my father's spectacular marriage failures and she was rebounding from a long-term relationship. With hindsight, I can see neither of us was in a good place. But we got on okay and we drifted into a relationship that probably looked more stable from the outside than it actually was. But I guess I wanted everyone to think that. I didn't want to be seen to be switching partners faster than I changed shirts.'

'But you were together for three years. No one would've accused you of being fickle if you'd ended things at two years or even at a year,' Abby said.

'I know, but there never seemed to be a good time,' he said. 'I almost called an end a couple of times earlier but then Kimberley got news of her ex getting married and then of him becoming a father. It was a tough time for her.'

'Oh, Luke, you sound like you were an amazing partner.'

'That's me.' His voice was both self-deprecating and bitter. 'A regular Mr Perfect.'

Abby decided it was time to share some of her own guilt, so he didn't have to feel so alone and isolated. Nothing was more isolating than guilt. She should know—she had graduated with Honours from the Academy of Guilt. 'I have a few regrets on how I handled things with my mother. I wish I'd been able to get help for her sooner but she died before I could.'

'I didn't realise she'd actually died. What happened?'

Abby let out a long breath, wondering if she was wise to reveal any more. People were funny about drugs and prostitution. Would it make him see her differently? Make her appear even more unacceptable to him than she already felt? But in the end she decided to tell him because of the trust he had shown in telling her about his guilt over his ex. 'Drug over-dose. Heroin. She stuck the needle in her arm and died in the next room.'

Shock rippled over his features like wind through leaves. 'How old were you?'

'Five. But I remember it as if it were yesterday. I've always blamed myself. What if I was a difficult child? Too much for her to handle. What if I drove her to take that overdose?'

'You were five years old, for pity's sake,' he said. 'It was her responsibility to look after you. What could you have done anyway?'

'Maybe checked on her earlier…' Abby blinked, trying not to think of that day. Even though she had been so young, the image of coming out of her bed-room the next morning and seeing her mother lying on that threadbare-carpeted floor was imprinted on her brain.

Luke came over to her and placed his hands on her shoulders. 'Look at me, Abby.'

Abby slowly brought her gaze back to meet his. 'Even though I was young, I remember a lot about the night before she died. I was tired and hungry and my mother was agitated and insisted I go to bed earlier than usual. She would often lock me in there when… Anyway, she must have injected herself while sitting on the floor by her bed because that's where I found her the next morning. I would have got help earlier if I'd realised what she'd done. That's what I have to live with. I could have saved her but I didn't. The irony is my bedroom door wasn't even locked. I just thought it was, like it had been so many times before. I went to bed and went to sleep, thinking it was better than having a big showdown with her where she would hit or slap me. When I came out in the morning, I thought she was asleep but she wasn't...'

'Oh, Abby.' He gathered her close in a hug, his arms warm and supportive and protective as if he were holding that small, terrified child and comforting her.

That was all he said: *Oh, Abby.* But within those two words was a message of understanding and empathy that she hadn't realised until now she had been waiting all her life to hear.

After a few moments, he eased back to look at her with a soft and tender look that made her heart swell like bread dough. 'You mustn't blame yourself.'

'Ditto.'

He made a rueful movement of his lips and stepped away from her again. 'Yeah, well, do as I preach but not as I do. Hypocritical of me, I know, but that's the way it is.' He walked into his en suite bathroom and came out with his bathrobe. 'Here. Put this on for now.'

Abby took the bathrobe from him and went into the bathroom to put it on, expecting when she returned he would have left the bedroom, but he was back over by the window, staring at the dappled sunlight coming through the leaves of the tree outside.

'Luke?' She took one step towards him and then two and then four until she was standing with her arms wrapped around his waist from behind.

His hands came down on hers and she braced herself for the moment he would push her away but it didn't come. Instead, he turned and his hands went to her hips, holding her close enough for their bodies to brush. 'This is crazy.' His eyes went to her mouth as if he had no control over his vision. 'Stupidly, irresponsibly crazy.' And then his mouth came down and covered hers.

CHAPTER SIX

A THRILL RUSHED through Abby at the undercurrent of passion in Luke's kiss. His lips moved with increasing urgency against hers, drawing from her a response that was equally passionate. Her body came alive at the determined thrust of his tongue, sending an electrifying shockwave of lust through her, making her bones shudder with the force of it like someone rattling a loosely assembled cage. His tongue found hers and played with such blatant eroticism her inner core contracted with greedy, hungry need.

This was why she hadn't made love to anyone before. No one had ever made her feel this level of arousal. No one had made her feel wanted for *her*. Not just for her body. He made her feel safe and understood. Desire shot through her with hot darting arrows, making her aware of every secret crevice of her body in a way she never had before.

The hollow ache between her legs became unbearable. A pulsing ache that begged for the possession of his hard body. An ache that could not be satisfied by anyone but him.

Luke walked her backwards to the bed, his mouth still fused to hers, the movement of his thighs brushing against hers making her insides quiver in feverish anticipation. No kiss she had ever experienced made her feel this level of excitement. Every one of her erogenous zones was eagerly awaiting his touch. She could feel herself swelling in her most secret place, the tingling sensation like a hollow spasm of part pain, part pleasure.

Luke laid her down on the bed and came down beside her, his hand going down her body in one slow stroke from her breast to her thigh and back again. When he came back to her breast he bent his mouth to it, circling his tongue around her tight nipple, stirring sensations in her that made her back arch like a cat enjoying a stroke.

He opened his mouth over her nipple, teasing it with his tongue, and then drawing on her with gentle little sucks that made her mouth drop open on a gasp of pleasure. He moved to the other breast, subjecting it to the same exquisite torture, sending riotous pulses of delight through her body.

'You're beautiful,' he said against her lips. 'Every inch of you is so damn beautiful.'

Abby wasn't used to receiving compliments and wasn't sure if he was just saying it to make her feel more comfortable with him. But she already felt amazingly comfortable with him. Why else had she stood half naked before him without a qualm? 'Careful,' she said with a self-effacing smile. 'You'll give me a big head.'

'That's not the only thing that's getting big around here.' His crooked smile made his blue eyes glint.

'I can feel it.' Abby reached for him, taking him carefully in her hand so she could explore the shape and heft of him. He was beading at the tip, the signal of high arousal, and it thrilled her to think she had done that to him.

He groaned and then let out a swift breath and eased her hand away, holding it captive in his. 'I don't want to rush this. To rush you.'

Abby was so aroused she couldn't imagine needing further stimulation. But when he brought his mouth back to her breasts her desire went up another notch, until she was breathing heavily as his lips and tongue and the gentle pressure of his teeth made her body sing like an opera diva.

He moved from her breasts to press soft just-touching kisses all the way down to her belly. He dipped the tip of his tongue into the shallow whirl of her bellybutton, setting off a racing fire of need further down her body.

'I want to taste you.' His voice had that honey and gravel combo thing going on. She hadn't realised it was possible to be so turned on by a man's voice.

Abby had read about this type of pleasuring but had never thought it was for her. She thought she'd be too shy or embarrassed at being so exposed to a lover. But, strangely, she felt none of that. All she felt was a sense of rightness, that this was what she wanted and needed, and somehow he did too.

He kissed her mound, allowing her time to get

used to him being so close to the most intimate part of her body. Then he gently opened her with a stroke of his tongue, the caress making her shiver from head to foot with a cascading shower of powerful sensations. He went deeper, his lips and tongue working on the swollen nub of her clitoris, sending lightning strikes of pleasure through her.

The sudden orgasm swept through her like a hurricane through a house of cards, spinning her senses, flipping and rolling and tossing them until her entire body was shaking with it. Ripples of aftershock pulsed through her flesh, leaving her breathless until every muscle relaxed as if her skeleton had been turned to liquid. 'That was…amazing isn't the right word,' Abby's voice came out as a whisper. 'Mind-blowing. Unbelievable. Magical. Wow. Wow. Wow.'

He came back to kiss her mouth, the musky taste of her on his lips exciting her in a way she would never have thought possible. It added another layer of intimacy that made her feel as if something had shifted between them.

Something unique and special that could not be undone.

Luke caressed her breasts again, lingering over each one as if he couldn't get enough of her.

'Aren't you going to—?' Abby said, feeling the hard ridge of his arousal against her thigh.

'I'm trying to slow down.'

'You don't need to. I'm ready.' She was more than ready. Her body was crying out for the physical connection that would finally join her with him in the most intimate embrace known to humankind.

He framed her face with his hands, his gaze searching. 'Are you sure about this. Really sure?'

Abby had never felt surer about anything. 'Make love to me, Luke. Please?'

He took in an uneven breath, his gaze dipping to her mouth, his thumb pad stroking along her lower lip. 'You have such a kissable mouth. I've thought about kissing it for a long time.'

A rush of pleasure ran through her. 'How long?'

'Remember when Ella first introduced us?'

'Yes.' Abby remembered it well. It had been four years ago when she was nineteen and still trying to find her feet. She had not long started a journalism degree because she couldn't decide what course to take and she'd met Ella while she had been working part-time in a bookshop to cover her study expenses. They'd struck up a conversation about the books they liked and within no time at all they were catching up for coffee and chatting as if they'd been friends since childhood. Not that Abby had told Ella the truth about her childhood. She wanted to maintain the image of herself she always projected, as someone who didn't have baggage or hang-ups or embarrassing relatives she would never have chosen if she'd had a choice. 'Ella brought me around to your house to meet you.'

'I wasn't in the mood for visitors.'

'I could tell that,' Abby said. 'I didn't like you at all. I thought you were standoffish and gruff.'

He stroked her bottom lip again, his gaze still trained on her mouth. 'I didn't always use to be like that... Well, not that bad, anyway. But when you smiled at me that day it made me feel about a thousand years old.'

She stroked her hand down his chest to his erection. 'You don't feel that old to me.'

He gave her a twisted smile. 'You're still way too young for me.'

'I'm only nine years younger and I'm mature for my age, or at least I like to think so.' Abby considered herself mature because for as long as she could remember she had been thrown on the mercy of her own resources. Nothing made you grow up faster than having no reliable adults around to depend on.

He kissed the end of her nose. 'You have an air of youthfulness about you. Like you believe life is meant to be fun and happy and you'll do anything you can to make it that way.'

'It's called positivity,' Abby said. 'Looking forward not back.'

His eyes did that searching thing again as if he was looking for something in her gaze. 'Abby...' He touched her face with a brush of a finger. 'You need to understand this is only for now. I can't promise more than that and even a short time frame is probably risking things.'

Abby wasn't sure what exactly he thought he was risking. Liking her too much? Enjoying being with her? Maybe even falling in love with her? But there was her risk assessment to consider. What if *she* fell in love with him? Was she flirting with danger by entering into a short-term affair that had no possibility of being for ever?

'We can set a date if you want,' Abby said, repeating her offer from earlier. 'We can programme it into our phones to give us a reminder. *Ping.*' She snapped her fingers. 'End of fling.'

A flicker of something passed through his gaze. 'You're joking, right?'

'I'm not joking,' Abby said. 'This is clearly creating a bit of stress for you so why not both of us agree on a breakup date?'

'It sounds a little...clinical.'

'It's more practical rather than clinical,' Abby said. 'We agree on a date and stick to it. Seriously, I should write a column about this. I could call it the no-nonsense guide to having a fling, or a fling without tears.'

His expression was shadowed by a frown and he started to ease away from her. 'Maybe this isn't such a great idea.'

Abby laid her hand on his arm. 'So you get to pleasure me but I don't get to pleasure you? How is that fair?'

He placed his hand over hers, his mouth set in a firm line. 'All right. One week from today, okay?'

One week? Abby had been hoping for two, possibly three. Months, not weeks. Years would have been even better. 'Agreed.'

He held her gaze for a long beat before he bent

his mouth to hers, kissing her with such passion her desire for him hammered and hummed in her blood.

He lifted his mouth and reached for a condom in the bedside drawer, but she found it incredibly touching he had to rustle around in there for a while before he located one. His long drought between lovers made her feel even more special. This was a big step for her and it was a big step for him. They'd made a commitment to have a one-week fling. It was as if they were equals, two people on a search for connection on a purely physical level.

He looked at the small foil packet a little doubtfully. 'I hope this isn't past its use-by date. Are you taking any contraception?'

'I take the Pill so I can regulate my cycle,' Abby said. 'I hate getting my period at inconvenient times. The Pill means I can plan it to fit in with my lifestyle.'

He unwrapped the condom and applied it to himself and then came back to settle between her legs, one of his positioned over hers, his weight propped up on his arms. 'Still sure you want to do this? It's not too late to stop.'

Abby took his face in her hands and eyeballed him. 'What part of *I want you* do you not understand?'

He gave her another crooked smile. 'Okay. I get it. You want me, but I don't think you want me half as much as I want you.'

'Try me and see.' She moved against him, offering herself to him, going on instinct as if her body knew what to do and when to do it and all she had to do was go with it.

He parted her with his fingers, and then he gently inserted one finger. Once he was sure she had accepted him without flinching, he inserted two fingers, moving them ever so carefully against her flesh as if she were something infinitely precious. 'Still okay?'

'Wonderfully okay,' Abby said on a shuddering sigh.

He moved over her, positioning himself so he could enter her, taking his time so she could get used to her body wrapping around him. She gasped with pleasure but he mistook it for pain and pulled away, his expression taut with concern. 'Did I hurt you?'

'No, I was just taken by surprise by how good it feels, how good *you* feel,' Abby said.

He moved back to her folds, slowing entering her inch by inch until she accepted him fully. Then he began moving, slow and gentle thrusts that sent waves of delight through her body. It wasn't as direct and intense as when he'd pleasured her with his mouth, but the rhythmic movement of him stirred a pool of longing into a whirlpool. She was almost there but not quite, her body straining to reach the summit but unable to find the point of no return.

Luke reached down between their bodies and caressed her with his fingers in a flickering movement that triggered an explosion in her intimate flesh. It radiated out in rippling waves that flowed through her body until she was half crying, half gasping from the ferocious impact of it.

He waited until she was done before he gave a series of hard, quick thrusts as if he was unable to control the tempo now he had finally allowed himself to let go.

And then there was silence—a silence unlike any Abby had experienced before. Peace descended on her like the feathery down of a luxury quilt, covering her body in a mantle of exquisite relaxation…

Luke couldn't tear his eyes away from Abby, sleeping next to him. Her body was once more entangled with his; one arm flopped limply over his waist, the other hand resting on the *thud-pitty-thud* of his heart. He was in two minds about berating himself for what had just happened. What he had allowed to happen. But he couldn't quite bring himself to fully regret making love to her. The experience of holding her in his arms, possessing her and leading her to her first orgasm with a partner was beyond anything he had experienced with any other lover.

Was that why it had been so different, because Abby had been a virgin? He wasn't sure, although it had definitely given their encounter a special context that made him feel privileged and honoured that she had trusted him to be her first lover. He knew one thing for certain; he would never forget the experience.

But this was as far as it could go.

As far as he would allow it to go. A brief fling and

then it would be time for her to move on and find her Mr Perfect—if such a man existed.

Luke had been so shocked to wake up with her spooned against him. Deeply shocked in his mind and yet his body had hijacked reason, sabotaged his resolve and made a mockery of his determination to keep away from her.

God only knew what his sister would make of his week-long fling with Abby. Ella had been at him for years—at least four years—to get back out there in the dating pool. Unbeknown to his family, he had gone on a couple of lukewarm dates over the last couple of years. But he didn't take them any further because he was unable to invest in a relationship where he would be responsible—accountable—for someone else's emotions.

He'd seen first-hand the emotional devastation of his mother when his father left. It had been gut-wrenching to witness and his sense of utter powerlessness had always stayed with him. Luke had worried for years she would never recover. He had an overwhelming sense of responsibility to keep the rest of the family together. To keep his mother in good spirits even though it had been a difficult battle to this day. She had never re-partnered and in a way he couldn't blame her. He too had been blindsided by his father's abandonment of the wife and family he had claimed so volubly and so publicly to love.

Abby nestled closer like a little cub. Luke began stroking her wavy chestnut hair in rhythmic strokes, breathing in the scent of her, of their lovemaking. Wondering again if he was a fool to have given in to the temptation of taking their relationship to this intense level of intimacy even if it was only for a week. He had always kept his distance from her—from anyone when it came to that. Whenever Ella had visited him with her in tow he had been formal and yes, a little gruff on occasion, but the way Abby's big brown eyes lit up when she smiled had done something to him—something he'd found immensely threatening.

She was open and he was closed. She was warm and he was cold. She was fresh and funny and optimistic and he was stale and moribund and staunchly, immovably pessimistic.

But somehow Abby had melted his resolve like a blowtorch blasted at butter. His body was drawn to her by an irresistible force, like lightning was drawn to metal, and his pleasure had been just as earth-shattering. Had he ever felt satisfaction like it? Or had it been too long between drinks to tell with any certainty? It was like making love for the first time and yet so much better, because his first time had been rushed and clumsy and over all too soon.

This time, his pleasure had lasted for ages inside his body. He could still feel the slight hum of it lingering in his flesh like the rumble of distant thunder.

Abby moved against him again, stirring his blood into a deep throb of longing. She opened her eyes and smiled at him. 'Hey, did that just happen or am I dreaming?'

Luke brushed an imaginary hair away from her face, keeping his own expression a little less open, stilling each facial muscle as if he was folding down the four top sections of a box. 'It happened.'

A frown flickered across her brow. 'You already regret it, don't you?'

He traced a fingertip over her bottom lip. 'I'm concerned you're going to think this is more than what it is.'

'You mean more than just sex?'

'A week-long fling is a week-long fling, it's not for ever,' Luke said, carefully gauging her reaction to his words.

She gave a soft laugh. 'Who are you really worried about losing perspective on our one-week fling? Me or you?'

That was exactly what he was worried about. He had already blurred the boundaries he had maintained for so long. Crossed a line he couldn't uncross. He had given in to the desire he had long suppressed or ignored or been too busy to allow to become a priority.

He could not undo their lovemaking.

It would always be something they had shared. Something unique and special, something she would never experience with anyone else and, he suspected, nor would he. The uniqueness of it encased it in an impermeable membrane of memory.

'Cute theory, but no,' he said. 'I know what I'm capable of and commitment is not something I'm interested in.'

'But we're going to be exclusive, right? While we're together this week?'

Luke was faintly annoyed she felt the need to ask. Did she think he was the type of man like his father? That it was a case of like father like son? He lived by very different principles from his father, who had worked his way through several partners since his initial affair. 'Of course we'll be exclusive. You have my word on that.'

'You have mine too,' Abby said with a smile. 'I think it's cowardly to cheat on someone. Why not be honest and say you're not happy with how the relationship is going? It seems only fair, in my opinion.'

'I couldn't agree more,' Luke said. 'When my father cheated on my mother she had no idea. No inkling anything was wrong. Only the month before, he had taken her to a nice restaurant to celebrate their seventeenth anniversary. He'd even bought her flowers the week before.'

Abby's frowning expression showed her disgust at his father's behaviour. 'That's nothing short of cruel. What type of man is he? A sadist?'

'Yeah, well, I don't have too much to do with him these days,' he said. 'I can't bear listening to him bragging about his latest conquest, especially when I know another couple of his exes took it badly when he dumped them.'

She stroked his cheek, her soft hand catching on his stubble, her eyes luminous. 'You're a nice man, Luke Shelverton. A decent man with standards that put other men like your father and mine to shame.'

Luke's ears pricked up at the mention of her father. What she'd told him about her mother had shocked him to the core. She had seemed reluctant to discuss either of her parents with him the day before. He couldn't help feeling touched she had let him in on such a painful secret. 'He's alive then? Do you ever see him?'

She looked down at his chest, where her fingertip was following the line of his right collarbone. It was as if she was mentally preparing herself—each stroke and glide of her finger against his collarbone was somehow building up her courage. 'I haven't seen him since I was five and a half.' Her gaze climbed back up to his. 'Family Services thought it would be good for me to have a connection with him after my mother died, even though they'd split up and he hadn't had anything to do with me for months.'

Five and a half years old. Luke couldn't get his head around it. What despair and fear had she felt to see her mother lying lifeless on the floor. And how terrifying to be handed to the father who hadn't been there for her for months on end.

His gut churned with anguish for her. For the senseless suffering she had endured because of the incompetent adults who should have been loving and protecting her.

Luke gently cradled her cheek, his eyes meshing with hers. 'I'm so sorry you went through that. I can't imagine how terrified you must have been.'

She gave him a flickering smile that seemed sad around the edges. 'I don't think about it much now.

It was a long time ago and in some ways it feels like it happened to someone else, not me.'

'Is that why you've not told Ella? Because you've rewritten your history to make it less painful?'

'Less painful and less shameful,' she said. 'My father is in jail and has been since I was six. He almost killed someone on a drug deal that went sour. He was the one who got my mother on heroin, I'm sure of it. It came out much later he was the leader of a drug gang. But back then he made everyone think she was the one with the problem. He painted himself as the poor pushed-aside father of his child. And the authorities fell for it, for a time.'

'Did you feel any connection with him when you went to live with him?'

Abby shook her head. 'I hated him. He was bad-tempered and treated the new woman he was with like a slave. And he made her do most of the looking after of me, which of course she resented and took out on me. He only wanted me because he thought it would whitewash his reputation with the social worker who used to do visits. I felt uncomfortable with him and would always end up in floods of tears when the social worker came. He made it sound to the social worker that I was crying because I was upset at the thought of being taken away from him and put into permanent care. I was too frightened to tell them the truth because I was worried they mightn't believe me over my father. He could be so convincing. And then, if they didn't believe me and left me with him after I'd said something, I knew he would punish me for speaking out. I felt so powerless.'

Luke pulled her close as if he could somehow make up for the shocking way she had been treated. He might have some issues with his own father, but at least he had never been passed like a parcel between foster carers. He had always had his mother and felt secure in her love. He had his sister, who always did her best to make their fragmented family work as well as it possibly could.

But Abby had suffered for most, if not all, of her childhood. How could she have turned out to be such an open and warm and positive person? She deserved much better than she had received. Could he in some small way make up for all the heartache and despair she'd endured?

The thought started as a seed in his mind and then started to spread its roots, tunnelling its way into every closed-off corner of his brain like a rampant vine. He could take her on the island holiday. He could spoil her and treat her like a princess for a week. He hadn't had a holiday in ages and it would be a good way of getting to know her even better. Besides, her flat was still uninhabitable and was likely to be for a few more days. This was a perfect solution.

A faint alarm bell sounded in the back of his mind, but he disregarded it. It was only for a week and they had both agreed on that. He wasn't promising a future with her.

He couldn't promise a future with anyone.

Luke picked up one of her wayward curls and wound it round his finger, holding her warm toffee-brown gaze. 'It would be a shame to forfeit that holiday I won.'

A light came on in her eyes. 'Are you saying what I think you're saying?'

He gave her a slow smile. 'I quite fancy a week in the sun. I'll have to juggle a few things in my diary but—'

'Oh, Luke, thank you, thank you, thank you.' She pressed her mouth to his in a series of kisses, making his lips swell and tingle for more. 'It'll be so much fun. A whole island to ourselves.'

'How soon can you pack?'

Her face suddenly fell. 'But what about my flat? I can't get to my clothes and I don't feel comfortable wearing—'

'No problem,' Luke said. 'I'll go and buy you something you can wear so we can go and get the rest. My treat.'

Her teeth worried her bottom lip and her eyes didn't quite meet his. 'I'm not sure I'm comfortable with you buying me stuff.'

He tipped up her chin so she met his gaze. 'Listen to me. I want to spoil you. I'll probably enjoy it more than you, so why not allow me this little bit of pleasure in my boring and stuffy workaholic life?'

Her eyes had a spark of wickedness. 'I'm all for giving you pleasure.' She wriggled closer and linked her arms around his neck, bringing her mouth within touching distance of his.

Luke closed the tiny gap between their mouths, his senses on fire at the way her lips moulded themselves to his. He stroked for entry and she opened to him on a sigh that made the base of his spine grow warm. Warmth that spread its way through the rest of his body, sending his blood on a fevered flood to his groin.

He caressed her breast, cupping it and then stroking his thumb over its peaking nipple. He took his mouth off hers to attend to her breast, licking around her areola and gently grazing the nub of her nipple with his teeth. She made a breathless sound of appreciation and moved restlessly against him, searching for him with her hand beneath the fabric of his sleepwear and finding him fully erect. The feel of her fingers wrapping around him made him even harder, the need pulsing through him in electrifying waves.

She kissed her way from his neck in hot little presses of her lips against his skin, all the way down past his abs.

Luke sucked in a breath and placed a hand on her shoulder. 'You don't have to do that—'

Abby glanced up at him with doubt flickering in her eyes. 'But you did it to me. Don't you want me to—?'

'Abby.' He cradled her cheek in his hand. 'I don't want you to do things with me because you think you have to. I want you to be comfortable with every part of what we do together.'

'But I am comfortable. I'm more comfortable with

you than anyone I've ever met. Talking about my childhood… Well, I've only ever told you that stuff. That's how comfortable I feel with you.'

Luke was touched she felt that way. Deeply touched. And so turned-on he was holding on to his self-control like someone trying to control a wild stallion with a silken thread. His thumb stroked the curve of her cheek, holding her shining earnest gaze. 'Are you sure you want to do this?'

She reached for him again, caressing him just the way he liked it as if she had some secret way of reading his body. 'I want to make you feel the way I did when you did it to me.'

A part of Luke insisted he stop right there, but another part—the caged part that was primitive and primal—wanted her mouth. Wanted her tongue. Wanted. Wanted. Wanted until he was throbbing with it.

Abby didn't wait for him to talk her out of it even if that sensible and civilised part of him had been on active duty. She reached across him for a condom and unpeeled it from its packet. She wriggled down and pushed away his sleepwear but, before she put on the condom, she breathed her warm breath over his engorged length. It was like being caressed by the breeze of a moth's wing and intensely, spine-tinglingly arousing.

'Give me the condom.' Was that his voice? That husky croak that sounded as if it came from the middle of a frog pond.

She held it just out of reach. 'I can do it. I did this

once in Sex Ed. But I have to tell you, you don't look anything like a courgette.'

'Good to know.'

Once the condom was on, she brought her tongue to him in soft little licks like a kitten lapping milk, making him shudder with fizzing pleasure that spiralled through his body. She opened her mouth over him, moving up and down his shaft with varying degrees of suction, and he groaned and groaned and fought to stay in control, wanting to prolong the thrill of watching her pleasure him.

Fight it or fly? Fight it or fly?

The mental chant was in time with his pounding blood.

And then he flew...

CHAPTER SEVEN

ABBY HAD NEVER seen anything so erotic as Luke totally at her mercy. His guttural groans and whole body shudders made her feel a wave of deep pleasure as if his orgasm was somehow tuned to a sensitive radar in her body. Triggering little electric shocks deep in her core at the realisation of her sensual power as a woman.

Luke was lying on his back, his breathing not quite back to normal, and he took her hand and brought it to his mouth, kissing each fingertip in turn, his eyes holding hers. 'That must have been quite some Sex Ed class,' he said with a wry smile.

Abby laughed and lay across his body, toying with the short and fine whorls of his dark brown hair at the sides of his neck. 'I like seeing you smile.' She traced her finger around his mouth, her skin catching on his stubble like silk on an emery board. 'You're really funny behind that stern façade you put up.'

He gave her a mock frown and rolled her on to her back and pinned her with his weight, his dark blue eyes gleaming. 'Stern? Is that how you see me?'

Abby shivered with delight at the hard press of his erection against her thigh, so close to where she ached and pulsed with longing. She traced each of his ink-black eyebrows, smoothing out the semi-permanent frown line that was etched into his forehead. 'I like it when you smile instead of frown. It makes you more approachable.'

He smiled and leaned across to get another condom. 'I am going to have to restock soon or we're going to have a problem.'

The only problem Abby could see was that she was going to get too emotionally involved in this fling. It was a risk she had been prepared to take, but had it been foolish to think she could keep her emotions separate? Making love with Luke was not a simple matter of two bodies joining for mutual release. There was so much more to it. A bond of intimacy developed and grew with each and every encounter.

She could *feel* it happening.

Each kiss, each stroke, each caress bonded her to him in a way she could never bond with anyone else. He was her first lover. The man who had taught her about receiving and giving pleasure. The man who responded to her as if her touch and her touch alone could unlock the primal desires he had suppressed for so long.

Luke leaned on one elbow to apply the condom, giving Abby a perfect opportunity to stroke her hand down his chest and sexily toned abdomen. He eased her back down and brought his mouth to each of her breasts, tending to them with licks and strokes and grazes of his gentle teeth that made every cell of her body hum with delight.

Abby was so ready, so full of need she couldn't stop a pleading whimper from escaping. 'You're taking too long. I want you *now*.'

He gently parted her folds and entered her with a groan that seemed to come from deep inside him. Abby welcomed him into her body, wrapping her legs around his hips so he could deepen his thrusts. The smooth, slick glide of his body within hers set off sparks in her nerves that swelled and sensitised her clitoris. But it wasn't quite enough friction to trigger the orgasm she could feel building like a rampaging storm in her female flesh.

Luke reached down between their joined bodies, caressing her with an expert touch like a maestro handling a Stradivarius. She soared off into the stratosphere, her mind partially blanking out as the ripples and shudders ricocheted through her body.

Abby floated back to reality just as he started to increase his pace, the faster, deeper thrusts triggering his own release. He gave a choked-off sound and then emptied in a series of pumps, finally collapsing over her, his head buried next to her neck.

She played with his hair in little lifts and tugs of the thick dark brown strands, listening to his breathing steadying, the rise and fall of his chest against hers making her feel closer to him than she had felt to anyone.

Luke turned his head to nibble at the sensitive

area below her ear, making her shiver all over. 'You're amazing. You know that, don't you?'

Abby turned her head so she was eye to eye with him, his breath mingling with hers. 'I was just thinking the same, but about you. My theory was right then.'

He sent his finger on a slow journey around her mouth. 'Which theory was that?'

'The dancing one,' Abby said. 'If a couple are good on the dance floor together, then they're likely to be good in bed together. We've just proven it.'

His smile did strange things to her insides, making them gooey and soft like melted marshmallows. 'Do you have any more theories you want to run past my sceptical scientific brain?'

Abby squinted her gaze. 'You think I'm nuts, don't you?'

He captured her mouth and pressed a hot, hard kiss to her lips. 'I think you're beautiful and funny and I'm going to make love to you all over again. That is, unless you'd rather dance?'

Abby pulled his head back down to hers. 'We can dance later.'

Later that morning, Abby had a shower and waited for Luke to come back with a casual outfit for her to wear and some underwear. It gave her a little thrill to think of him choosing knickers and a bra for her. Handling those intimate items with his clever hands, knowing he would be the one to take them off her when they next made love.

Abby wandered through Luke's house, a part of her feeling guilty at snooping, but the other part wanted to know everything about him. He was like a really gripping book she'd started reading and couldn't put down. She'd got him to open up about his girlfriend Kimberley…although she felt a little guilty her back story had overtaken the telling of his. Had that been deliberate on his part? Using her little trick by taking the searchlight off his life and shining it on hers?

Abby didn't regret telling him about her background. She'd thought she would but somehow she didn't. Luke was a safe person to tell. There hadn't been too many safe people in her life. But he was trustworthy and dependable, exactly like Ella, which meant Abby would have to tell her at some stage too.

But then, as if summoned by the thought of her friend, Abby's phone rang and she picked it up and saw it was Ella. 'Hi, I was meaning to call—'

'Is it true?' Ella said, excitement ringing in her voice. 'Luke actually went with you to the ball?'

'Yes, I finally got him to—'

'It was a rhetorical question, silly.' Ella laughed. 'I've seen the pictures of you from last night. They're all over Twitter. Don't you make quite the stunning couple?'

Abby wasn't sure she was ready to tell her friend *everything* about her and Luke. Like how her body was still humming from his lovemaking like a struck tuning fork. 'It was a fun night. Your brother is a surprisingly good dancer.'

'Oh. My. God.' Ella gasped. 'You got him to dance? Really?'

'Yes. We had heaps of fun and we even went out and had supper afterwards.'

'Are you serious?' Ella's voice was rich with delight. 'What else did you two get up to?'

Abby retreated into a protective silence. How could she just blurt out what had happened between her and Luke, even if it was to her best friend?

'Oh. My. God,' Ella said when the silence went on too long. 'Don't tell me you actually *slept* with my brother?'

'We—ell...'

'But that's marvellous!' Ella's voice wasn't far off a squeal. 'He hasn't slept with anyone since Kimberley. I'm sure of it. He hasn't even been on a date that I'm aware of. Well done, you.'

'You mean you...you don't mind?'

'Why should I mind? It would be a dream come true if you and he—'

'Don't get too excited.' A strange little pang struck Abby in the belly. 'We're just having a one-week fling.'

'Fling, *schming*,' Ella said. 'You're not the type of girl to have a fling. If you were, you would've had one by now. You certainly haven't had one since I've known you, otherwise I would have known about it. Are you sure you're doing the right thing? I mean it's great Luke's getting back out there, but a week isn't long enough for either of you to—'

'Ella…there's a lot of stuff you don't know about me…'

'You mean stuff about your childhood?'

Abby's heart missed a beat. 'What do you know about my childhood?'

'Just that you don't like talking about your family. You always change the subject or get me talking about myself instead. I see you doing it with other people too. You shift the focus off you.'

'Why haven't you said anything about it until now?'

'Because I figured you'd tell me when you were ready,' Ella said. 'You're not close to your family, are you?'

'That's because they're not my family.' Abby filled her friend in on most of what she'd told Luke. And, just like when she'd told him, a little more weight went off the burden she'd been carrying for so long.

'I wish you'd told me earlier,' Ella said. 'Poor you—having such a horrible childhood. But I can see why it would have been difficult for you to talk about, even to me. It's kind of nice you told Luke first, though. He's always been a good listener.'

'He's good at lots of things.'

'Speaking of which, fling or no fling, I think it's brilliant you and he are getting it on. It's what you both need.'

'Are you sure you don't mind?'

'Why should I?'

'But what if it makes things uncomfortable in the future?' Abby said. 'Like when I'm with you and

Luke is present once this week is over. It could be awkward for everyone.'

Most especially me.

'Think of it this way,' Ella said. 'Your fling with Luke will be a positive thing, no matter how it works out. It will help him move on.' There was a tiny pause. 'But you have to be careful, you know. Don't get your hopes up in case—'

'You don't have to worry about me,' Abby cut in with far more confidence than she felt. 'We've agreed it's only going to be for a week. No one is going to fall in love in that time.'

'I'm not so sure you can predict that with any certainty because—'

'Enough about me,' Abby said. 'How's school going? How were the parent teacher interviews?'

'I know what you're doing, Abby, but this time I'm going to let it slide,' Ella said. 'You don't want to talk about it, so fine. We won't talk about it. But please be careful. Luke has a thing about commitment. I think it comes from having a father like ours.'

'I'm sure Luke is nothing like his father.'

'He's not, but that doesn't mean he'll change his mind about settling down,' Ella's voice had a note of warning. 'I know what my big brother is like. Luke is so stubborn he could be conducting workshops and tutorials for mules.'

Abby couldn't help smiling. 'Believe me, I know.'

Luke bought an outfit and some lingerie for Abby at a boutique in Bloomsbury and walked back to his house, but he couldn't help feeling conflicted. Making love with her was amazing. Amazing and fulfilling and unlike anything he'd experienced before. But he couldn't quite dismiss the niggling worry he was stepping out of his comfort zone.

Way, way out.

Letting someone close, *that* close, was like peeling back the edges of a wound and preparing for the lightning strike of pain. So far it hadn't happened. So far. But how soon before it did? Letting someone into his life made him uneasy. As if he was walking over a lake of ice and not being sure where it was thick and where it was thin, every step a potentially dangerous one.

A potentially lethal one.

Abby had got under his guard like someone slipping under crime scene tape while the forensics team turned their backs. He had told her things he had told no one. But then so had she revealed things about herself to him that were painfully private.

Her disclosure made him feel…trusted. Yes, that was the word he was looking for. She trusted him with the truth about her difficult background. The shameful truth she had deliberately and desperately hidden behind a complicated web of white lies, like a magician using smoke and mirrors to fool the audience.

Abby's seemingly perfect life was exactly that— just an illusion.

So what the hell was he doing getting stuck in the middle of it? Pretending to be her Mr Perfect. Taking her on a luxury holiday for two like a freaking romantic honeymoon.

What was he *thinking?*

That was the trouble when he was around Abby. He didn't think. His body took over his mind and every primal desire in his system pumped and pounded and pushed against his willpower like a bulldozer against a cardboard box.

Because he couldn't resist her.

That first kiss had been his downfall, the second splintering his self-control like a sledgehammer on glass. Those kisses had flicked a switch inside his body, making every attempt on his part to withstand the potent lure of attraction a dismal failure.

Abby was his kryptonite. His peanut. He had to have more and more of her because it was impossible to resist her.

And for the next week he wasn't even going to try.

Abby had never been on a shopping spree before where someone else footed the bill. Shopping for herself was usually a tricky business of balancing her bank balance with her constantly overstretched credit card. She knew she couldn't really blame her background on her issues with money. In spite of her parents' woeful example, she had witnessed her various foster families balance delicate budgets and still provide meals and essentials, although not too many luxuries. She had great intentions of saving but something would always crop up—another bill, a friend in need, a charity she just had to make a donation to because she perceived their need to be greater than hers.

But when Luke took her shopping there was no question of her whipping out her credit card. He took care of everything and was a surprisingly helpful shopping wingman. And he was great at carrying all the bags.

Abby was in a boutique with him where there was swimwear as well as other casual fashion items. She ran her hand along the row of hanging bikinis and wondered if she had the courage to wear one. She had always worn a one-piece because it held in her less than toned stomach.

'Why don't you try one on?' Luke said.

Abby dropped her hand from the rack. 'I don't have the figure for it. I'd be too embarrassed.'

'There won't be anyone else but us on the island so what's to be embarrassed about?'

She turned back to the row of colourful bikinis in the section where her size was located and sighed. 'I don't know...'

'Here.' He reached past her shoulder and took three bikini sets off the rack: a black one, a vividly hot pink one and a bright canary-yellow one. 'You'd look great in any of these. Go on. Try them on.'

Abby took them from him but she was still feeling uncertain. 'Do you really think—?'

Luke bent his head to just near her ear. 'Personally, I'd prefer you totally naked, but yes, I think you'll look fabulous in all three of them. Now get in there and try them on.'

She shivered at the erotic promise of his words and the way his warm breath caressed her skin. She gave him a mock salute. 'Yes, sir.'

His dark eyes glinted and he gave her a playful pat on the behind. 'Cheeky minx.'

Abby went into the changing room and peeled off her clothes, trying to see her body in the mirror as Luke saw it. Since her early teens she had struggled with body image. The rush of hormones in puberty had turned her boyish figure into a lushly womanly one but she hadn't been emotionally ready for the impact it would have on the male gaze. Comments and leering looks from men had triggered some of the memories of her mother's clients and it had made her ashamed of her body instead of proud of it.

But when Luke looked at her she felt none of that shame. Almost from the first time she'd met him her body had been aware of him, but not in a threatening way. The way his gaze would drift to her mouth had given her a secret thrill that in spite of his standoff-ish demeanour he found her attractive.

Abby turned this way and that in front of the mirror, cupping her breasts in her hands, remembering how it felt to have Luke hold and caress them. Just thinking about him touching her sent another frisson through her.

She lowered her hands and tried on each bikini, unable to make a choice between them. She got dressed back in her clothes and, carrying the bikinis, came out to where Luke was waiting for her.

'How did you go?'

'I like them all but—'

'Good, then we'll take them all.' He took them from her and handed them to the hovering shop assistant. 'We'll take these.'

The young female assistant smiled at Abby once the bikinis were paid for by Luke and wrapped in tissue paper and placed in the shop's signature bag. 'Wow, he really is a perfect fiancé. I love your column, by the way. Your advice is always spot on.'

'Thank you,' Abby said, taking the bag's cream satin ribbon handle.

'Oh, is that your engagement ring?' The assistant peered across the counter at Abby's left hand. 'Can I see it?'

Abby lifted her hand for inspection but, looking at the ring, she realised it wasn't the sort of ring Luke would buy his fiancée if he ever had one. It was too flashy and cumbersome and it didn't really suit her hand. It was a *nouveau riche* type of ring— the sort of ring worn by someone trying too hard to impress. It was a status symbol, not a ring about the relationship status itself. She held out her hand and was excruciatingly conscious of Luke standing silently beside her.

'It's lovely,' the assistant said. 'I hope you'll both be brilliantly happy, but then of course you will. You're the perfect couple.'

Abby couldn't get out of there fast enough and was glad when Luke took her hand and walked her out of the shop. 'How about a coffee to finish up?' he said.

'I think I need something stronger than coffee.'

'That ring you're wearing is a cliché.' He turned the bulky setting around on her finger. 'And it's not even a real diamond.'

'How do you know it's not real?'

'It's a good fake, I'll give you that.'

Abby gave a self-deprecating grimace. 'I would've bought a real one if I'd had the money.'

His mouth tilted in a smile. 'You're a funny little thing, aren't you?'

'Yes, well, that's me—a living, breathing joke.'

A frown pulled at his brow. 'Hey.' He lifted her chin again, his intelligent blue gaze warm and darkly intense. 'I'm not laughing at you, sweetheart. I like your quirkiness. It's refreshing.'

Abby's heart gave a stumble. 'You just called me sweetheart.'

His hand fell away from her face. 'Wasn't that the deal? To call you terms of endearment in public? Honey and babe and sweetheart. Those were the correct words, right?'

'Yes…'

'But?'

She shrugged. 'I just didn't think you'd do it, that's all.'

His eyes held hers. 'Why's that?'

'You don't seem the type of man to say things you don't mean,' Abby said.

'You can thank my father for that.' He took her hand and continued walking with her down the street. 'He was big on words and small on action. I sometimes wonder what my mother saw in him. He doesn't seem her type at all.'

'I have heaps of readers who fall for the wrong men,' Abby said. 'It's like some women are programmed to choose the worst possible partner for them. And some do it repeatedly.'

'Thing is...' Luke paused. 'I think she's still in love with him, even after the way he humiliated her. I don't get it. Who does that?'

A woman in love.

'I guess there's no accounting for chemistry,' Abby said. *Isn't that the truth?* 'When it strikes it strikes and there's little you can do to stop it.'

CHAPTER EIGHT

THEY CONTINUED ALONG the street until they came to an exclusive cocktail lounge Abby had heard heaps about but never visited. Luke led Abby inside and they were soon seated at a velvet-covered sofa in a private corner.

Abby swept her gaze over the beautiful décor and wanted to pinch herself. She'd always wanted to come in here but it had always been out of her price range.

'What do you fancy?' Luke asked, handing her the drinks menu. 'A cocktail and peanuts or something more substantial?'

What I really fancy is you.

'Gosh, this place is amazing. Look at the list of food. And I've never heard of some of these cocktails. It makes me want to try them, just to see. I guess my diet can wait another day.'

He gave Abby a mock stern look. 'If I hear you say the word *diet* ever again I will not be answerable for the consequences.'

Abby gave him a quizzical look. 'You don't believe in diets?'

'Firstly, diets have a woefully high failure rate,' he said. 'Most people lose weight and as soon as they stop the diet they put it all back on again and more. And, secondly, you look fine just the way you are.'

'Thank you for saying that.' Abby reached across the table for his hand. 'I've struggled for years with body image.'

His warm, strong fingers wrapped around hers, sending a wave of longing through her. 'You have a beautiful body.'

She gave him an on-off smile and lowered her gaze to their joined hands. How nice would it be if a ring Luke had bought her was on her finger instead of that ridiculous fake?

After a while the waiter brought their drinks and a tasting plate of delicious food to share. Abby sat back and started on her cocktail, which seemed to go straight to her head, or maybe that was because of the way Luke kept looking at her as if he was reliving every moment of their lovemaking. She looked at the pattern around the edge of the tasting plate rather than meet his gaze. 'I guess not having parents around who loved me unconditionally has messed with my self-esteem.'

'Understandable, given what you've been through.'

Abby sighed. 'I've always been a bit jealous of Ella, you know. Growing up with two parents, well, at least one highly functioning one and a big brother to boot. That's why I made up so much stuff about my background and never told her the truth. As far as I'm concerned, that girl with the dodgy parents no longer exists.'

His eyes were warm with understanding. 'I think you underestimate Ella, but I hear what you're saying.' A shadow drifted through his gaze. 'I haven't told anyone I broke up with Kimberley that night. No one but you, that is.'

Abby put her cocktail glass down. 'Do you think she told anyone? I mean, before she got…?'

'Not that I'm aware of.' He shifted the base of his cocktail glass a quarter turn. 'There was a window of a couple of hours after she left my place and the accident. She might've just sat in her car and cried, for all I know.'

Abby could understand why he felt so crushingly guilty. How could he tell everyone they had broken up two hours before Kimberley's tragic death? What would it have achieved except more hurt for the poor girl's family? And, even if he had told them, wouldn't it have heaped even more blame on his shoulders that he didn't deserve? Couples broke up every day. Every minute or second across the world, people were ending their relationships. How could Luke have possibly known by ending his relationship with Kimberley she would be involved in a car crash a couple of hours later? It just wasn't possible.

And it certainly wasn't his fault.

But it made her realise how deeply sensitive Luke was underneath the gruff front he presented to the world. He'd thought deeply about how Kimberley's family would suffer even more heartache if they thought he had no longer wanted to be with her.

'Was she terribly upset when she left your place?'

His features clouded with the memory. 'That's another thing I've never really understood. She wasn't all that upset. I got the feeling she knew I was going to end things that day. I even thought she seemed... I don't know...relieved somehow. And yet...' He gave his head a little shake. 'Maybe I just wasn't good at reading her mood. I keep asking myself, did I *listen* to her? Did I hear what she wasn't saying instead of what she was?'

'Maybe in that two-hour window she talked to a friend,' Abby said. 'That's usually what women do when they're upset. They go to their girlfriends for support.'

'If she'd told anyone then no one mentioned it at the funeral or since,' Luke said. 'That's been one of the hardest things, apart from the guilt. Her family see me as the grief-stricken partner, unable to move on.' He gave a quick twist of his mouth. 'Thing is... It seems to help them to think that. They find it comforting that someone other than them is still devastated by her death.'

'But you are still grieving,' Abby pointed out. 'It's a process, not a timeline. You move through each of the stages when you're ready. Some people take years, others a lifetime and some never get through it. There's no right way of doing it.'

His smile was a wry slant. 'I can see why you

landed that job of yours. That's a wise head on those very beautiful shoulders.'

Abby shrugged off his comment and eyed the last olive on the tasting plate. 'Aren't you going to eat that?'

He pushed the plate across the table. 'It's all yours.'

Luke went to his London office first thing on Monday morning and shuffled his diary around and in the process gave everyone on the staff a minor heart attack at his uncharacteristic spontaneity. It was weird, but no one at his office seemed all that surprised that he was 'engaged' to Abby Hart. They bought it just like everyone else who had access to a phone or computer screen or newspaper.

'I always thought you were a dark horse, Luke,' Kay, his middle-aged secretary, said with a teasing smile. 'But I couldn't be happier for you. I love Abby's column. I read it every week. Her advice stopped me divorcing John last year.'

Luke frowned. 'I didn't know you guys were having trouble.'

Kay flickered her eyes upwards in a don't-get-me-started manner. 'I was going to leave him because he'd stopped helping me around the house and would just sit on the sofa in front of the TV while I buzzed around doing everything. But Abby pointed out in her column, most couples don't get divorced over a basket of washing. There are usually bigger issues that are hiding under the dirty laundry. She was bang on the money. Poor John had some financial worries from his business that were making him depressed and moody and tired. He was too ashamed to tell me about them, and if it hadn't been for Abby's advice I still might not know. That girl is a genius.'

Luke couldn't hold back a smile. 'She is pretty special, isn't she?'

Kay's beaming smile rivalled a set of sun-soaked solar panels. 'Well, look at you, smiling for the first time in I don't know when.' She leaned forwards and rested her forearms on her desk, her expression now sober. 'I guess you kept your relationship with Abby a secret out of respect for Kimberley's family. But they must be happy for you, surely? It's been five years.'

Luke's gut did its usual sharp claws clench when he thought of Kimberley's family. He'd called them to explain his engagement to Abby wasn't real, that it was just a favour he was doing for her. He hadn't told Abby he'd told them that because she was so insistent no one knew her fiancé was a fake. But he couldn't allow Kimberley's parents to hear about his 'engagement' from another source, especially in the press. 'Yes. I told them.'

'Well, even if you hadn't, you'd have to be a fossil hiding under a rock not to have heard about the outing of Abby Hart's Mr Perfect,' Kay said with another smile. 'Thing is, how on earth did you two keep it a secret for so long? That's taking dark horsemanship to a whole new level.'

Luke kept his expression safely in neutral. 'Believe me, it wasn't easy.'

* * *

Luke was on his way back to his house, where Abby was waiting for him before they headed to the airport, when he walked past a high-end jewellery store. He stopped outside and looked at the window display for a moment, realising it was totally out of character and that he was crossing a line he had never crossed before. But he couldn't stop thinking about her showing that shop assistant her ring the other day and how it had seemed to embarrass her. Why shouldn't he buy her something she wouldn't be embarrassed wearing? It was a way to make sure she was treated the way she deserved to be treated. It would also make him less conflicted about putting such a short time frame on their fling. He pushed open the door and asked to see the diamond pendant in the window. And once he had purchased the pendant he continued on his way home.

Luke was a little shocked at how much he was looking forward to this week on the island. Not just because he hadn't had a holiday in…when *had* he last had a holiday? It was so long ago he couldn't remember where he'd gone.

One thing he did know—he'd gone alone.

But a week with Abby on a private island was the stuff of fantasies. He couldn't help feeling excited about it. Hugely excited. Not just because their lovemaking was so freaking amazing, although he wouldn't be worthy of his testosterone if he didn't get hard just thinking about her in his bed. It was because Abby was fun to be around. She made him smile and he could barely remember the last time he'd smiled before she came barrelling into his life and demanding he be her Mr Perfect.

Luke was the last person to consider himself perfect, especially in an intimate relationship, but he couldn't help enjoying playing the role of her fiancé as it gave him the freedom to do and say things he wouldn't normally feel comfortable doing.

He wasn't a touchy-feely person. He wasn't the life-of-the-party loquacious type. He would rather design a robot than speak at length to a real person. At least he could program a robot to do what he wanted it to do.

But for some reason, with Abby, none of that mattered.

He liked the differences between them. He liked her laughter and her lightness of personality. He liked how she was positive and had such a can-do attitude. Her resourcefulness was a little wacky at times, like pretending to be in a relationship when she had never been in one before, and then giving everyone relationship advice that actually worked. Not to mention setting a date on when a fling should end. You didn't get much wackier than that.

Luke wanted this week on the island to be perfect for her. To make up for all that had happened in her childhood. He wanted to spoil her and make her feel like a princess for the next week.

Only a week?

He elbowed the thought away. A week was what they had agreed on.

And he was going to enjoy every smoking-hot second of it.

CHAPTER NINE

THE PRIVATE ISLAND and luxury villa were even better in the flesh than in the photographs, Abby decided when they arrived. Stunning views of the sparkling blue sea and the white sandy beach that fringed it could be seen from the sun-drenched terrace in front of the villa. A gorgeous infinity pool was set on the other terrace, which overlooked another fabulous view of the ocean. There were beautifully manicured gardens situated about the villa, and the slightly peppery scent of the scarlet pelargoniums that were in terracotta pots and hanging baskets filled the air.

The warm air with its hint of sea salt caressed Abby's face when she lifted it to the sun and she closed her eyes for a moment, taking in the distant cry of a seabird and the twittering of the birds in the nearby shrubs. She opened her eyes to see Luke smiling at her. 'What?' she said, suddenly embarrassed.

He gave her pony-tailed hair a gentle tug. 'You're so easily impressed.'

'Who wouldn't be impressed by this?' She waved her hand to encompass their surroundings. 'This place is amazing. Pardon me for being a little over-whelmed but I've never been on a private island be-fore. Nor have I seen a place as fabulous as this. Apparently the villa has won several architectural awards and I can see why.'

Luke gave a cursory look at the villa. 'It's not bad.'

'Not bad?' Abby laughed. 'You're the master of understatement. I would like to see something that does impress you.'

'You in one of those bikinis I bought you would impress me,' he said with a glint in his eyes.

Abby's core coiled and contracted with need. 'That can be arranged as soon as I unpack.'

Luke opened the front door of the villa with the key he had been given by the person who had brought them to the island by boat. She still couldn't believe they had the island to themselves for the week. Not even any of the household staff were on the island this week. The housekeeper and gardener and pool maintenance people were on leave. However, gour-met food and boutique wines and champagnes had been left as part of the prize package, and the boat operator had informed them fresh fruit and vegeta-bles would be brought in by boat mid-week.

Abby followed Luke inside the villa and couldn't stop a gasp escaping when she saw the interior of the foyer. The walls and floor were polished marble and a Swarovski crystal chandelier hung from the ceiling in prisms of glittering light like a fountain of shim-mering diamonds. The large windows allowed the view to come in from each side of the villa, making it seem even more spacious and spectacular. Three sides of the villa overlooked the sea but the fourth side overlooked the densely wooded forest of the hilly area on one side of the island.

Luke had a floor plan in the folder he had been given by the boat operator, but Abby was too impatient for that. She went on her own tour of discovery, calling out to him when she found another delightful room or stunning angle of the house.

'Look at this, Luke.' She pointed to the well-appointed kitchen and the breakfast room that opened on to a terrace where jasmine hung in a scented arras from the side of the villa. 'I can't wait to cook in there. And we can eat outside whenever we want.'

'It's a holiday. You're not meant to cook.'

'But I want to cook.' Abby all but drooled at the luxury appliances and the acres of marble workspaces, which made her cramped kitchenette look like a shoebox. A baby's shoebox. She opened a butler's pantry. 'Goodness me, you could park a car in here it's so big.' She closed the door and grinned at him. 'Am I gushing too much?'

His slow smile made something in her stomach drop. 'Come here.'

Abby walked across the kitchen to where he was standing, her breath snaring in her throat when he slipped a hand to the nape of her neck. His eyes were so dark a blue his pupils almost disappeared. 'I don't want to waste a second of this holiday with you slaving over a hot oven.'

She linked her arms around his neck and leaned into his hard frame, her body tingling at the erotic contact. 'So you'd prefer me slaving over your hot body instead?'

The glint in his eyes intensified. 'I couldn't have put it better myself.' His hands settled on her hips, holding her against the pulse of his body. His mouth came down and covered hers in a long, drugging kiss that made the backs of her knees feel fizzy. A hot pool of longing opened up inside her, creating a whirlpool deep in her core.

Abby sighed against his mouth, weaving her tongue with his, her body tingling with the need to get closer. Luke's hands were already working on her clothes, peeling them from her body as if he was unwrapping a present he had been waiting to open for a long time.

'I want you,' he said, moving his mouth against the sensitive skin of her neck, the caress of his warm breath sending shivers down her spine.

Abby was suddenly conscious of how hot and sticky she was from their travel. 'Maybe I should shower first…'

'I have an even better idea.' He took her hand and led her out to the sun-dappled infinity pool on the terrace.

There were towels in a hamper under a shelter and he took two out and laid them on two sun loungers. There was even sunscreen in a spray bottle thoughtfully placed nearby.

Then he undid the rest of his shirt buttons, looking at her with such explosive erotic intent her legs threatened to give way. 'Ever skinny-dipped before?'

Abby shook her head. 'I've always been too shy to do something like that.' Not to mention she was a hopeless swimmer. She only ever stayed in the shallow end because she hadn't learnt to swim with anything remotely near proficiency.

He stepped out of his trousers and shoes and socks and underwear before he came back to help her with the rest of her clothes. With each article he removed, he left a kiss in its place, his lips and tongue moving over her flesh in little nudges and licks that made her desire for him swarm through her body in a hot wave.

The sensation of the sun on her naked skin was so sensually arousing but, teamed with Luke's kisses and skilled caresses, she was breathless and aching with need within seconds. 'Are you sure no one can see us?' she said, sliding her hands down his muscular chest.

'We're totally alone.'

Abby glanced nervously towards the ocean in the distance. 'What about on the water? Maybe there's a yacht with a stonking big telescope that will—'

'Abby.' Luke's voice had a soothing quality to it that was like a caress in itself. 'You're safe with me. I wouldn't bring you out here if I didn't think it was private.'

Was she safe?

Safe emotionally?

Abby brushed aside the thought. She wasn't falling in love with Luke. That wasn't part of the deal.

How could she fall in love so quickly anyway? She was confusing phenomenal sex with love. Hadn't she written a column about that once? It was a classic mistake people made, especially women, confusing great sex with love, often being disappointed when the novelty wore off, to find there was nothing underpinning the relationship but physical lust.

Luke picked up the sunscreen and sprayed her back and shoulders and then handed her the bottle to do his. Once they were safely covered with sunscreen, he brought her back to the cradle of his body, his hands sliding down to cup her behind, his mouth fusing to hers in a searing kiss that made her toes curl against the sun-warmed flagstones. Then he lifted his mouth off hers to blaze a trail of kisses down to her breasts, subjecting each one to licks and sucks and gentle nips that made her gasp with delight.

After a moment, he lifted his mouth off her breast to nod towards the pool. 'Time to cool off?'

Abby glanced at the markings on the floor of the pool. 'Can we stay in the shallow end?'

'You're not confident in the water?' He framed it as a question but it sounded more like an observation, especially since he was looking at her in an understanding manner.

'Well, let's put it this way,' Abby said with a self-deprecating grimace. 'Every time I try and swim, someone throws me a flotation device and calls for a lifeguard. Swimming lessons weren't a priority at any of my foster placements.'

'Then that's something I can help you with while we're here.'

'Ella told me you won a heap of medals during your schooling but you stopped swimming when your parents split up,' Abby said.

A shadow passed over his features. 'Yeah, well, club training wasn't a priority after that.'

'Because you were always too busy looking after your mum and Ella?' Abby asked.

He made a twisted movement of his mouth. 'Don't get me wrong. I was glad to help with Ella. She was a good little kid and no bother. I just missed out on the stuff other teenagers my age were doing. It made me feel like an outsider. But I guess you know all about feeling like that.'

'Sure do. But I think what you did for Ella and your mum was amazing. They're so lucky to have you.'

He gave her a quick smile. 'Let's get you in the water before you melt, okay?'

Abby was so hot from his caresses she was expecting the water to sizzle when she entered it, holding Luke's hand for support. And the only melting she was going to do was when he looked at her with his dark blue eyes full of smouldering desire. The water enveloped her in a blessedly cool embrace that felt like silk against her naked skin. Maybe swimming wouldn't be so scary after all.

Luke brought her close to the aroused length of his body. 'There's only one problem with making love in water.'

'Putting on a condom?'

'Yep.'

Abby bit her lip. 'I guess we could go without...'

He looked at her for a long moment. 'No can do. Too risky.'

Abby knew he was being responsible about having safe sex. She was always insisting on her followers doing the same, but a part of her—a secret part— wished he would relax his rule for her. 'Because this is just a fling, right?' She tried to tone down the bitter note in her voice but didn't quite pull it off.

He let out a gust of a breath and slid a hand down one of her arms. 'Abby... Think about it. If you were to get pregnant it would—'

'I know, I know, I know,' Abby said. 'It would be a disaster for you.'

He frowned. 'And for you too, surely?'

Abby kept her expression blank while her mind suddenly raced off with images of her holding a baby—a little dark-haired angel with deep blue eyes. She blinked away the image and pasted a smile on her face. 'Of course it would be a disaster. I'm still building my career. I don't want to have kids until I'm in my late twenties at the earliest.'

Luke's expression was guarded, as if he wasn't sure whether to believe her or not. 'The Pill is mostly reliable but I don't want to risk it.'

'It's fine, Luke, really,' Abby said. 'I've written heaps of columns about this. It's too easy to get lost in the heat of the moment and then it's too late to undo. I've had heart-wrenching letters from followers who've had to deal with an unplanned pregnancy, more often than not to a guy they no longer want anything to do with. You're being sensible and responsible and I'm grateful for it.'

He gently tucked a wispy strand of hair behind her ear. 'So, swimming lesson first and then we'll finish this later.'

An hour later Abby wasn't quite ready for the Olympics but she could get from one end of the pool to the other without ending up with a lungful of water. The pool contained saltwater, which added extra buoyancy, and with Luke's excellent coaching she was reasonably confident she wouldn't drown if she stepped out of her depth.

She completed another lap and stood at the end and blinked the water out of her eyes. 'How many have I done now? I lost count.'

'You've done enough for one day,' Luke said. 'Besides, the sun is starting to pink your skin. The sunscreen's probably washed off by now.'

'I'll sit in the shade for a bit,' Abby said. 'You've been so patient with me but you must be dying for a swim yourself. Go on. I'll enjoy watching you. It'll be like watching a training video.'

Abby covered herself with a towel and sat on one of the sun loungers and watched Luke glide through the water with such economy of movement and graceful skill it was a delight to watch. He tumble-turned at each end with supple agility, and even more delightful was seeing all of his powerfully sculpted muscles coming into play. The strong back and shoulders, the long and muscled legs, the toned arms, the clever hands that were placed at just the right angle to maximise propulsion through the water. He had the sort of skin that tanned rather than burned, and even in the short time they'd been out here in the pool his skin had darkened.

After a few laps, Luke propelled himself out of the water by his hands on the edge of the pool. Abby sucked in a breath as the muscles in his arms and on his abdomen contracted at the movement. He wasn't the slightest bit uneasy about being naked, but then she wasn't uncomfortable being naked with him either. Physically or emotionally, which was even more surprising. She had told him more about herself than she had told anyone. Was it because he was a good listener or was it because he too had suffered? Whatever the reason, it gave them a common ground on which to communicate.

Luke came over to where she was sitting and perched on the end of her sun lounger near her feet. He shook his head like a wet dog and sprayed water droplets all over her legs.

'Hey—' Abby laughed and gave him a playful shove '—get away from me.'

He leaned over her, anchoring his arms either side of her waist, his eyes dark and gleaming. 'Are you sure that's what you want?'

Abby touched his lean tanned jaw with her hand, his dark regrowth grazing her fingertips. She looked into the bottomless blue of his eyes and knew in that moment the last thing she ever wanted was to have him away from her.

She wanted him close.

As close as she could possibly be to him. Wasn't she already closer to him than anyone? Her eyes fell away from his to study his mouth instead. She traced it with her fingertip, memorising it so she would never forget its sexy contours. 'You have a nice mouth. Strong and firm and masculine and yet soft too.'

He captured her finger with his mouth, drawing on it like he had suckled on her nipples. 'I'm rather fond of yours too,' he said once he released her finger. 'As you've probably noticed.'

Abby gave him a half smile. 'Do you think when this week is over we will still be able to be friends?'

A frown flickered over his forehead. 'I don't see any reason why not.'

'I know…but these things have a habit of becoming complicated…'

He pushed up her chin once more, locking her gaze with his penetrating one. 'Are you having second thoughts?'

Abby made sure her choice of words wouldn't betray her doubts. 'No. It's just it gets tricky running into exes at family gatherings and stuff. I mean, Ella is practically family to me and you too, so—'

'It won't be tricky, okay?' He stood from the sun lounger so quickly it nearly overbalanced. One of his hands scraped his damp hair back with such force it left deep groove marks along his scalp. 'I'll deal with it. We'll both deal with it like adults.'

'I don't see why you're so upset,' Abby said. 'I'm just expressing concern about how we're going to handle this going forward. We both have to be clear on how we're going to handle it.'

'Are you trying to ruin this holiday?' He glared at her so heatedly it made the bright sunlight seem dim by comparison. 'Is that what you're doing? Because if so it's working. We've only got a few days. Let's not waste them by worrying how we're going to look each other in the eye at Christmas and Easter, okay?'

Abby bit her lip. 'I'm sorry…'

He let out a long slow breath and came back over to sit beside her. He took one of her hands and brought it up to his mouth, pressing his lips against her bent knuckles. 'I'm sorry too.' His eyes were soft again. 'I shouldn't have spoken so harshly. Forgive me.'

'I shouldn't have pressed your buttons.'

He tucked another strand of her hair back behind her ear. 'Your nose is pink.'

Abby screwed up her face. 'I hate you for being able to tan without tears. I go pink and then I peel and get more freckles. Go me.'

He sent his fingertip down the slope of her nose. 'Your freckles are cute.'

She smiled and touched his mouth again with her fingertip. 'Are you going to finish what you started before we had a swim?'

He got off the lounger and pulled her to her feet. 'I'm all for a bit of alfresco sex but I don't want you to get sunburnt or the rest of our week will be ruined. Let's go inside.'

'Sounds like fun.'

He pressed a hot kiss to her mouth. 'I'll make sure of it.'

Luke woke from a relaxing post-sex snooze to find Abby had disappeared from the bed beside him. He could see the indentation of her head on the pillow and the tangle of the bedclothes from when they had made passionate love. He glanced at his phone on the bedside table for the time and was a little shocked to see a couple of hours had passed. He could hear sounds of activity in the kitchen downstairs and smiled to himself at the thought of Abby bustling about in there as if it was her idea of a good time. His approach to food was purely functional. He ate when he was hungry and he stopped when he was full. But he suspected that came from long years of living alone.

Luke's mind drifted back to his conversation with Abby by the pool. He wasn't sure what her motive was in talking about them running into each other in the future. Had she wanted him to consider the fact that she was bound to meet someone else and make him jealous at the thought of her bringing a new man home to meet his family? Why would he be jealous? She had a perfect right to get on with her life once their fling was over.

That was the deal—one week and one week only.

But the thought of running into her with a new partner made something in his stomach twist. Would he have to go to her wedding? Would he have to stand

and watch some other guy promise to love her and stay true to her for the rest of their lives?

Not going to happen.

Luke came downstairs to find Abby laying a table on the terrace overlooking the ocean. She was dressed in one of the casual outfits he'd bought her on their shopping spree and her hair was on top of her head in a loosely arranged knot that gave her a bohemian hippy look. She glanced up from folding a napkin and smiled. 'Nice sleep? I checked on you an hour ago and you were out for the count.'

'You should have woken me.'

She made a mock pout. 'Uh-oh, you're frowning. Maybe you should have stayed in bed a bit longer.'

It's no fun if you're not there with me.

Luke would never say it out loud because he didn't even like thinking it. It would be admitting he needed her. He didn't need anyone. He made sure of it. 'What can I do to help with dinner?'

'You can open the wine, or should we have champagne?'

'What would you like?'

'Champagne,' she said, eyes shining. 'This is my first ever private island holiday, well, yours actually since I'm gatecrashing.'

'I was happy to bring you,' Luke said. 'It's good to see you enjoying yourself.'

She gave her lower lip a nibble and started fussing with the flowers she had arranged in the middle of the table. 'Actually…there's something I need to ask you…'

'Yes?'

She turned from the table with a sheepish look. 'I got a text from Felicity. She wants me to post some pictures of us on our holiday on my Twitter and Instagram feed.'

Luke didn't even have to think about his answer. 'No.'

Her face crumpled with disappointment. 'But surely a couple of photos won't hurt? It will make—'

'You can post photos of yourself if you must but please leave me out of it. No way am I going to have my photo plastered all over social media.'

'You didn't seem to mind the night of the ball.'

'That was different,' Luke said.

'How is it different?' she asked. 'You were pretending to be my fiancé then and you're pretending now. What's a few more photos going to do?'

'None of this is real, Abby,' Luke said. 'You. Me. Us.'

Her brown eyes flinched as if he'd struck her. 'But our fling is real...isn't it?'

'Yes. For one week and one week only.'

'Fine. I'm okay with that,' Abby said, folding her arms across her body. 'I just don't see the problem with taking a few photos and sharing them online.'

'Look, you might be happy about sharing your life with the rest of the planet but I'm not,' Luke said. 'Once that stuff is out there you can't take it back. It's out there for ever.'

She chewed her lower lip as if she was thinking

about something. 'I guess it might be a bit awkward for Kimberley's family...'

Luke set his mouth in a flat line. 'It's not about her family. They know this is a fake engagement.'

Her eyes rounded in alarm. 'You *told* them about us?'

'I couldn't let them find out in the press,' Luke said. 'I thought it was better to give them the heads-up that it was a charade to spare their feelings.'

'But what about *my* feelings?' she asked. 'What about my job? What if they told someone it was a charade? What then? Did you think about that? My career will implode if they spill anything to the press. How could you do that without asking me first?'

Luke released a weary sigh. This was why he stayed out of relationships. He was rubbish at handling people's feelings. He hurt them without even trying. 'Look, I admit I should have discussed it with you first. But they're discreet and will keep it to themselves.'

'They'd better because otherwise I'm never going to forgive you if this blows up in my face.' She folded her arms and glowered at him. 'So...no photos. Is that your final word?'

'I just prefer to keep my life private. It's no one's business but mine.'

Worry flickered through her gaze. 'But what am I going to say to Felicity?'

'You could tell her the truth,' Luke said with a wry look.

Shock flashed over her features. 'I can't do that. I could lose my job.'

'You're going to have to tell everyone some time.'

She unlocked her arms and shifted her gaze. 'I know. I have it covered. I'm going to do a breakup blog. But don't worry; I won't make you sound bad. I'll make it that I broke it off because of my issues not yours.'

Luke came over to her and placed his hands on her shoulders. 'Look, how about I take some photos of you instead? How's that for a compromise?'

She seemed to mull it over for a moment before she let out a breath. 'They'd better be pretty damn good photos.'

He leaned down to press a kiss to her forehead. 'They will be.'

CHAPTER TEN

AFTER DINNER, ABBY sat with Luke in the moonlight on the terrace. He had taken several photos of her over the course of the evening and all of them were good. Some of them even brilliant. He had a good eye for lighting and with the golden and muted light during twilight and sunset he had made her look almost beautiful.

But she couldn't help feeling disappointed he didn't want to be in the photos with her. What harm was there in a photo or two? At least it would be something she could keep after this week ended. Would it have hurt him to allow her one little keepsake photo? She had no childhood photos to speak of. This was another reminder of how alone she truly was.

But she didn't want to be alone any more.

Not after this week. Not after being with Luke and experiencing the passion of being in his arms. Why couldn't they extend their fling? Why wouldn't he broaden the time frame to see how well they worked as a couple? Sure, they had little disagreements, but that was normal and even healthy. His refusal to be in the photos was a reminder of his unwillingness to commit to anything long-term and her stupidity in secretly hoping he would change his mind. How many times had she written about this in her column? Women always thought they could change men but it nearly always ended up in heartbreak. People could only change when they believed they had to change, when they felt the need to change. When they *wanted* to change. No one else could force you or coerce you.

'More champagne?' Luke held up the bottle.

Abby covered the top of her glass. 'Better not. I already feel a little tipsy.' Who knew what would come out of her mouth if she allowed her self-control to slip?

I'm in love with you. I want to be married to you and have your babies.

How could she have thought she could settle for a fling when all she wanted was for ever with Luke? She wanted to grow old with him, to bring up a family with him, to do all the things with their little family she had missed out on as a child. But how could she tell him that? It was the last thing he wanted to hear. The last thing he wanted was a permanent commitment. How could it have taken her this long to realise she loved him? Or had she been lying to herself all this time?

It was ironic but for years she had been telling lies. Heaps and heaps of little white lies and yet the one time she wanted to tell the truth she couldn't. If she told Luke how she felt about him he would be furious. Falling in love was never part of the deal. She had talked him into the charade and now she had to endure the clock ticking on their fling.

He sat back in his chair and looked at the wrinkled moonlit sea below. 'This place makes you wish you didn't have to go home.'

'Tell me about it,' Abby said, thinking of her cramped little flat and the thin walls where she heard her neighbours arguing or listening to their too-loud televisions. Out here in this paradise, all she could hear was the occasional cry of a seabird and the whisper of the wind through the cypress pines.

And that wretched ticking clock...

After a moment, Luke reached into his pocket and put a square box on the table between them. 'This is for you.'

Abby stared at the jewellery box, her heart beating so fast she was sure it was going to bounce out of her chest. 'What is it?'

'Open it and see.'

She picked up the box and prised open the lid to find a gorgeous diamond pendant winking at her from its bed of lush cream velvet. 'Oh, my goodness...'

She lifted the fine white gold chain and the diamond swung with sparkling brilliance as if someone had plucked a star out of the night sky.

'It's beautiful. I've never seen anything so gorgeous.'

She looked up from the pendant, trying to stop herself from getting emotional. No one had ever bought her anything so wonderful. It wasn't just that it was expensive, but more that he had gone out and bought it for her as if she was someone special to him. Someone he thought worthy of a beautiful, timeless diamond.

'But I don't understand... Why did you buy it for me?'

He gave a loose-shouldered shrug. 'I walked past a jewellery store and saw it in the window.'

Abby looked at the pendant and blinked back tears. But it was impossible for her to control the bubble of emotion in her throat. She gulped and clutched the pendant against her chest, trying to re-gain her composure.

Luke leaned forward and took her hand. 'Why are you crying? Don't you like it? We can exchange it for something else if you'd—'

'Oh, Luke—' Abby half-sobbed, half-laughed '—I adore it. I'm crying because no one has ever bought me something so gorgeous. I'm used to get-ting hand-me-downs or charity shop gifts. This is the most perfect present I've ever received. It's very generous of you, but you have to stop spending so much money on me.'

He rose from the table and came around to her side to help her put the pendant on. His fingers sent shivers through her body when he fastened the catch and then he dropped a light kiss to the top of her head before he came back to sit down opposite her. 'It's just a trinket. A keepsake to remember me by.'

A keepsake to remember him by.

The words were a wake-up slap to Abby's momentary slip into happy-ever-after dreamland. 'I'm not sure I'm going to forget you in a hurry.' She touched the necklace with her fingers. 'The last few days have been…the most amazing of my life.'

He smiled with one side of his mouth. 'I'm glad you're having a good time. You deserve it.'

'Are *you* having a good time?'

He took her hand and entwined her fingers with his. 'I'm having such a good time I'm going to have trouble getting back into gear for work.'

She squeezed against his fingers. 'Maybe you should schedule in a few more holidays.'

He turned her hand over and traced a lazy circle in the middle of her palm, his gaze following the movement of his finger, the gentle caress triggering a firestorm in her blood. 'Maybe I should.' After a moment, his gaze came back to hers. 'I used to love going on holidays before my parents divorced. But afterwards…well, it just wasn't the same.'

'It must have been so hard for you and your mum, trying to make things nice for Ella,' Abby said.

He released her hand and let out a jagged sigh. 'Mum tried her best but she found it hard to see other couples on holiday, other families doing all the things she used to do with us before my dad left. It was painful to witness her distress. I had to step up and do the man-about-the-house stuff—not that my father was any great handyman or anything—but on top of school work and looking after Ella, well, there wasn't a lot of time left over for hanging out with friends and doing normal teenage stuff.'

'You've been an amazing son and a wonderful brother, Luke,' Abby said. 'Your mum and Ella are always saying how much they adore you and wish they saw more of you.'

'I know I should see them more often but I'm always snowed under with work.'

'Maybe you allow yourself to be snowed under,' Abby said. 'You run a very successful business. Surely you can delegate or outsource a bit more so you can have a life as well as work? It's not healthy trying to do it all yourself.'

A frown knitted his brows. 'I enjoy work.'

'But you might enjoy other things too,' Abby said. 'But how will you know unless you free up some time to do them?'

He reached for her hand again. 'Okay, Miss Hart. We have the next few days for you to teach me how to kick back and relax. Are you up for it?'

Abby gave him a high five. 'Game on.'

Luke was having such a good time relaxing with Abby—and, yes, having fun...that word he'd almost forgotten existed—that he forgot to charge his phone until two days before they were to leave the island. But when he gave it some juice he was a little horrified to see all the missed calls from his office in London. He called to find out there was a crisis with one of the major projects he had going. But what was even more shocking to him was how close he had been to unplugging the charger and ignoring the long list of text messages and emails.

'You don't have to rush back,' his secretary Kay said. 'It can wait a day or two. We just thought you'd better know in case—'

'Of course I have to come back,' Luke said. 'I'm responsible for the project. I know all the codes and I can fix this in a snap. I can't allow anything to go awry at this late stage. I'll get the next available flight.'

'But what about your holiday with Abby? Don't you want to stay? You could do the recoding over the phone or on Skype or email them through.'

Luke did want to stay, which was the scariest thing of all. He never wanted to leave the damn island. He never wanted to leave Abby. But he had to. He was only making it harder on them both by allowing it to get this far. What had he been thinking? He couldn't just drop everything and hang out on a beach and have picnics and make love at sunset. That stuff was for other people. People who hadn't been stalked by tragedy and left to carry the guilt like an anchor in their gut. He had responsibilities and people relying on him. 'No,' he said. 'I'm coming back. This is far more important than a holiday.'

After five days of swimming and snorkelling and plunging into the sea from a rock face, Abby was constantly balancing the scales of having fun with the harsh reality the fun was going to end once the week was over. Making love on the beach, sunset picnics watching the night sky appear star by star, planet by planet, long candlelit dinners and lazy breakfasts had made the days pass faster than she wanted them to.

Luke had taught her to fish—something she had always wanted to do—and she had taught him to relax. They had two more days on the island before they returned to London, which meant their fling would be over.

But Abby had a feeling Luke might be rethinking the time frame. She'd seen him looking at her when he thought she wasn't watching with a thoughtful expression on his face. And he often toyed with the diamond pendant around her neck when he was lying beside her, letting the chain slip through his fingers and the diamond rest against his palm.

Was she imagining his change of heart? She didn't think so. She hoped not. She prayed not. Didn't the last few days prove how good they were together? She had never seen him smile so much and the tight lines bracketing his mouth and the creases on his forehead had all but disappeared.

Why wouldn't he want to stay in their relationship when they were so comfortable together?

Abby was putting the finishing touches to dinner when he came in carrying his phone and his overnight bag and frowning. 'What's wrong? That's the first frown I've seen you give for five days.'

'Sorry, Abby, but something's come up at work,' he said. 'I have to go back early. No one else can fix it but me and it's not something I can do over the phone. I've called the boat operator. He'll be here in half an hour.'

Abby's heart sank and the strings on her hopes severed. 'But what about me?'

'You can finish the holiday on your own. There's no point rushing back with me now, as I'll be stuck in the office for the next week by the look of things. You might as well make the most of the last couple of days.'

'But it won't be the same without you,' Abby said. 'What will I do with myself? There's no one else on the island.'

'I'll arrange for someone to be with you. A staff member or—'

'A *staff* member?' Abby stared at him. 'Why would I want to be here with a staff member when I only want to be with you?'

His features were set in tight lines. 'Look, I don't have time for this right now—'

'Make time, Luke,' Abby said. 'This is important to me. You can't just dash back to London as if the last few days didn't happen. Didn't they mean anything to you? Don't *I* mean anything to you?'

He let out an impatient breath. 'Look, if you're worried about what people are going to say then I can't see the problem. I'm not in any of the photos you post online so how will they know I'm not here with you?'

'But *I* will know,' Abby said. 'I'll be here wishing you were with me because…because I love you.'

He flinched as if she had hit him. 'Stop it. Stop it right now.'

'I won't stop it,' Abby tried to keep her tone calm. 'I can't hide it or pretend any more. I love you. The last few days have cemented it for me. I don't want our fling to end when the week is over. I want to be with you for ever.'

The frown between his brows brought all the tense lines back to his forehead. 'I told you what I was prepared to give you and a future wasn't a part of it.'

'But I think deep down you want what I want,' Abby said. 'You want it but you feel you don't deserve it because of what happened to Kimberley.'

'This has nothing to do with Kimberley,' he said. 'You're shifting the goalposts because you've had a great time playing in the sun and the sand, but it's not real, Abby. None of this is real. It hasn't been real from the start. It's just one big charade and I foolishly went on with it because—'

'If you say because you felt sorry for me I will scream loud enough to break all the windows,' Abby said. 'I don't want your sympathy. I want your love.'

Luke's phone rang and he put his bag down on the floor.

'Don't answer it,' she said. 'Surely this is way more important than a stupid phone call?'

He threw her an exasperated look and turned his back and answered his phone. 'Yes, I'm on my way. Yes. It's all under control.' He ended the call and turned back around as he pocketed his phone. 'I have to go.' He picked up his bag. 'There are people waiting for me.'

People far more important than her. He didn't say it but then he didn't have to. He had shown it by his choice to leave her here all alone. He hadn't asked her to go with him. Why not? It wouldn't have taken her long to pack. No, he wanted to leave without her because he had never been here with her. Not willingly. Not wholeheartedly.

'You were never truly here with me on this island, were you, Luke?' Abby said. 'Your refusal to be in any of the photos is proof you weren't with me in every sense of the word. I might as well have had a cardboard cut-out of you because that's all you give of yourself. The outer shell but not the innermost part of you. The part that wants what everyone else wants: love, connection, a future, a family. You've locked that part of yourself away and thrown away the key.'

'Abby.'

'Don't use that lecturing voice with me,' Abby said. 'I hate it when you do that. Why didn't you ask me to go back with you? No, don't answer that. I'll tell you why. You want out of this fling, don't you?'

'I never wanted to be in it in the first place.'

His coldly delivered statement was like a sledgehammer on the thin ice of her hopes. Each word caused a deep fissure in her heart until she could barely draw breath. 'Right, well, that's it in a big fat crinkly nutshell,' Abby said. 'Sorry for all the trouble I've caused you.' She unclipped the pendant from around her neck and handed it to him. 'Here. Take it back. The box is upstairs. I don't suppose you'll wait until I get it for you and pack up all the clothes you bought for me?'

'I don't want the pendant or the clothes,' he said through tight lips. 'They were gifts.'

'Oh, yes, for services rendered,' Abby said, casting him a look that could have frozen Mercury. 'Thanks, by the way, for helping me on that front. I'm sure my future partner will also be enormously grateful.'

There was a storm brewing at the back of his eyes but that was the only sign he was struggling with his anger. 'Enjoy the rest of your stay on the island.'

'Don't worry.' Abby inched up her chin. 'I will.'

Luke's flight was delayed heading back to London so by the time he got to his office one of his junior staff had solved the programming problem that had threatened his multimillion-pound project. He'd always thought Sanjeev had talent but this proved it beyond a doubt. He should've felt relieved everything was sorted, but with Abby's words still rattling around his brain like loose marbles he could feel another migraine coming on.

He didn't believe for a second she was in love with him. She was worried about her job and all the silly lies she'd told. They were two days from ending their fling and she was panicking about how she was going to maintain her reputation.

Well, that had nothing to do with him.

Not any more.

He shouldn't have stepped into the role as her Mr Perfect. That was his first mistake and the second was taking her to that island. A place like that, well, even he'd been a little set off course by all the fun they'd been having. He couldn't remember a time when he'd felt more relaxed.

But that didn't mean he wanted their fling to continue indefinitely. He'd toyed with the idea of extending it a bit. Sure he had. Why wouldn't he? But even if he had adjusted the time frame, ultimately he couldn't give her what she wanted. He hadn't been able to give it to Kimberley or any other woman he had dated in the past.

Why should Abby be any different?

He didn't want the fairy tale she wanted. She might carry on with that psychobabble she was known for, saying he was overcompensating with work or locking away parts of himself. Well, he was damn fine with locking away parts of himself. Those were the parts that had got him into trouble in the past.

He wanted none of it.

No wife.

No kids.

No commitment.

Abby had no right to insist he drop everything he'd worked so hard for just for the sake of the two days left of their holiday. He had responsibilities he took seriously. He had staff he had to provide income for and clients—important clients—and patients from all over the globe depending on him getting this exciting new project off the ground.

But you could have come back to London later...

Luke shut down the thought. That phone call had been a good excuse to cut short Abby's silly little fantasy. He'd done the right thing in coming back. Of course he had. Their fling had gone on long enough. He shouldn't have allowed it to start in the first place. He'd broken his own rule by allowing her to move in with him. And he never should have bought her that wretched pendant. What was it with women and jewellery? Abby had attached significance to his gift when all he'd wanted to do was give her something worth keeping instead of that fake stuff she wore.

Luke came out of his office just as his secretary Kay came in from a coffee break. 'Bet you wish you hadn't rushed back here now, eh?' she said. 'Sanjeev's a bright young man. We call him Mensa Man behind his back. You should let him do a bit more around here. He's more than capable.'

'I'm seriously thinking about it.' He turned back to go to his office.

'Was Abby terribly disappointed about having to come back early?' Kay asked.

Luke swallowed a tight knot. He wasn't ready to explain what had happened on the island. More to the point, he wasn't used to explaining his private life to anyone. That was Abby's forte. 'I left her to enjoy the last couple of days by herself.'

Kay looked at him as if he'd told her he had left Abby on the moon without a spacesuit. 'You left her behind? Alone?'

He shrugged. 'So? Only I needed to come back.'

'But why didn't she come back with you?'

'I didn't ask her to.'

'Why the hell not?' Kay asked. 'Did you have a tiff or something?'

Luke's throat was so tight he could have sworn he was wearing a tie but he still had on the casual shirt he'd dressed in on the island. He had to give it to Abby. She was a whole lot better at this lying gig than he was. 'It's...complicated.'

Kay crossed her arms and gave him the sort of look a mother did to a teenager who had failed an important exam. 'You've blown it, haven't you?'

Luke scowled. 'Can you quit the third degree? I pay you to work, not to pry into my private life.'

'You didn't have a private life before Abby,' Kay said. 'She's the best thing that's ever happened to you. Although I did wonder why she hadn't posted any photos of you from the island. That seemed a bit odd to me. I hope you weren't glued to your phone all the time. We tried to keep things ticking over here so you could relax, but then we hit that coding issue and—'

'What's odd about wanting my private life to be private?' Luke said with barely banked-down annoyance. 'I don't feel the need to tell everyone where I last had coffee or what I had for breakfast.'

'It's a way of connecting with people.'

'Yeah? Well, I prefer to do it the old-fashioned way.'

'Like that's been working a treat for you these last five years,' Kay's tone was so dry it almost crackled.

Luke drew in a savage breath and swung back towards his office. 'I knew I shouldn't have given you that last pay rise.'

'Do you want it back?'

He glowered at her over his shoulder. 'Keep it and your opinions to yourself. Understood?'

Kay saluted and clicked her heels. 'Yes, sir.'

Abby flew back to London the following day in such low spirits two of the flight attendants asked during the journey if she was all right. She mopped at her streaming reddened eyes and told them it was just an allergic reaction. When she came through Customs and saw all the couples being reunited it made her heart feel as if it was being crushed.

Why couldn't Luke love her? Why couldn't he want to be with her for ever? Why did he leave her to fend for herself like everyone she had ever loved had done?

There was no way she could have stayed on the island without him. Every corner, every space, every view contained a memory of their time together. All she had now was memories. She didn't even have any photos of them together because he'd been so darn stubborn about taking any. She'd sneaked a few of him when he wasn't looking, but there were none of them together. It was as if their time on the island hadn't happened, it was just a mirage.

Just like her life...

Abby couldn't avoid the truth any longer. For years she had been hiding behind a web of lies. Telling people who she wished she was instead of who she actually was. She wasn't the got-it-all-together girl of her blog and column. She was a lonely single young woman from a disadvantaged background who dreamed of having the fairy tale.

But her handsome white knight had locked himself in his tower of guilt and there was nothing Abby could do to change him. She shouldn't have even tried. If she had just come out with the truth in the beginning she wouldn't have caused herself so much heartache. So many times she had given people advice in her column but she hadn't taken it herself.

There was no way she would have told someone to pretend to be engaged to save face. She would have told them a relationship based on a lie wasn't an authentic relationship. What right did she have to give advice? Her life was a mess. It had always been a mess. Her whole life was a lie. And it had to change.

Right here.

Right now.

She took out her phone and started typing a new column. Felicity might hate her or even fire her for it, but at least Abby would no longer be living a lie.

Luke couldn't stop thinking about the island. The sun, the sand, the beach, the bay, and the rock they had dived from. The way the island cut out the rest of the world, created a safe haven where they had been in touch with nature. He couldn't stop thinking about the amazing food Abby had cooked and the long lazy meals where they had sat under the stars sipping champagne.

But most of all he couldn't stop thinking about Abby.

She was in his thoughts every minute and every

second of the day and night. She was in his body. He would close his eyes and feel her soft little hands moving over him. He could feel her mouth, her lips, her tongue. Her smile was imprinted on his heart. Every time he pictured her smile his heart would contract as if it was being squished between two thick books.

Every time he went home from work his house seemed emptier and lonelier than it ever had before. Even work wasn't as enjoyable and fulfilling as before. Especially with Kay shaking her head and casting him rolled-eyed looks all the time.

She'd stopped lecturing him but as he was leaving work that day he found Abby's latest column open on her computer screen. Luke had so far resisted the temptation to read whatever lies Abby was peddling lately, but this time he couldn't stop himself from reading. It wasn't a long piece but it was heartfelt and honest. In it Abby shared how she had grown up through the foster system because her parents had had drug and alcohol issues. She spoke of how desperately she had wanted to fit in, to be normal—all the stuff she had told him during their time together.

His heart ached for her, revealing all that to the public. It was such a brave and dignified thing to do, for she crafted it in such a way to help people who were struggling with the same issues as her parents so they didn't feel judged, but rather to let them know help was at hand. She went on to say her pretence over being engaged to Mr Perfect was something she deeply regretted because there was no such thing as a perfect partner. The only thing you could wish for was to be the best partner you could be and that love would take care of the rest, if you were lucky enough to find someone who loved you.

Luke read that line twice because his vision had suddenly blurred.

If you were lucky enough to find someone who loved you.

Abby loved him. Why had he found that so hard to believe? Or had he been too frightened to believe it? Too worried it wouldn't last or would be snatched away from him. But he had been the one to sabotage it. He had found someone to love him and he had left her behind alone. He hadn't even asked her to come with him when work called him away. He had made his work a higher priority than Abby.

But his only priority was Abby.

Hadn't the last few days demonstrated that? He was walking through life like a ghost. His life was meaningless without her sunny presence casting out all the shadows that had doggedly surrounded him for so long. Why had he been such an emotional coward? Had he ruined any chance of a future with her?

He wanted to see her straight away but there was one thing he had to do first. He should have done it years ago. He raced home to pack up Kimberley's things, shooting her parents a text to say he would be around to drop them off as soon as he got a chance.

He folded the clothes and placed them in a cardboard box and gently closed the lid. It was like closing a chapter of his life.

His phone pinged with an answering text from Kimberley's parents to say they were in the area—could they drop in for a minute to pick up their daughter's things? Luke was desperate to go and see Abby but he couldn't fob off Kimberley's parents. Surely he owed them a few minutes?

He opened the front door an excruciatingly long hour later to find Peter and Tanya Norman standing there. 'Come in,' he said, greeting them as he normally did with awkward hugs and handshakes.

Tanya looked like she'd been recently crying, but then that wasn't unusual. 'Luke…there's something I have to tell you. I think it's time to tell you the truth about what happened the night Kimberley was… killed.'

Luke looked at Peter but he was doing his stoic father and husband thing, although he reached for his wife's hand and gave it an encouraging squeeze.

'The thing is…' Tanya swallowed. 'Kimberley was going to break up with you. She was interested in someone else but didn't have the courage to tell you. She didn't cheat on you. I know that for a fact. She was just finding it hard to bring things to an end with you because you were always so good to her. I think the only reason she didn't tell you about it that night was because she felt like she had betrayed you by allowing herself to fall in love with someone else while still in a relationship with you.'

Luke couldn't get his brain around the bombshell

news. Kimberley had been about to leave him? No wonder he'd thought their relationship was past its use-by date. But he'd always blamed himself. 'Why didn't you say something before now?'

Tanya looked ashamed. 'I felt it would hurt you too much to know she had fallen in love with someone else. You were always so good to her. So kind and patient when I know she wasn't always an easy person to be with. But I think that's because she wasn't in love with you. She'd been so hurt by her last relationship and you were a safe person, someone she trusted to take care of her. But in the end she wanted more. She wanted what everyone wants. True love.'

Luke wanted to be angry but somehow couldn't summon the energy. Kimberley's parents believed he'd been in love with her. He didn't think it served any purpose to tell them he hadn't been. 'Thank you for telling me,' he said. 'It was very courageous of you.'

'I was worried when I saw you and Abby Hart had broken up,' Tanya said. 'I was pleased you had found someone. Really pleased. I thought I wouldn't be when the time came but I was. But then I felt terrible when I saw you'd broken up. I wondered then if it had anything to do with what happened with Kimberley. I couldn't let another moment pass before I told you what I should have told you years ago. She might not have loved you as you loved her but she did love you. It just wasn't the right sort of love.'

Luke opened his arms and welcomed her into a

warm hug. He reached out with one arm and included Peter as well. No one said anything. They simply stood in a circle of three, honouring their memories of Kimberley.

And for the first time in five years Luke felt an enormous weight lift off his shoulders.

Abby had been mentally preparing for the fallout after her column went live but the opposite happened. Her inbox was filled with messages of support and encouragement, her Twitter feed went nuts and Felicity even mentioned something about a pay rise.

But, even so, it didn't make her heart feel any lighter.

Ella had phoned her every day since Abby had been back in London but she had been surprisingly tight-lipped about her older brother, saying only that she was reluctant to take sides as they were both adults and had to figure out this stuff on their own.

But Abby was worried Luke might never figure out his stuff. His stuff had put his life on hold for five long years. Would he end up an old lonely man with no one by his side?

Would she end up alone?

Who else did she want but Luke? He was her Mr Almost Perfect. The man who had stolen her heart with his first frown.

Sabina came into Abby's office cubicle carrying a huge bunch of red roses. 'These are for you,' she said.

Abby's heart gave a stumble. 'For me?'

'Yep and there are more. Like heaps more.' Sabina nodded towards Reception. 'It's like a florist's shop out there. And a fruit shop.'

Abby frowned. 'Fruit?'

'Strawberries,' Sabina said, eyes twinkling. 'Chocolate-coated ones and champagne. A dozen bottles of it.'

Abby's legs were shaking so much she could barely stand and it was a moment or two before she could get her voice to work. 'Who's it from?'

Just then a tall figure appeared outside Abby's cubicle.

'They're from me,' Luke said and then proceeded to go down on one knee in front of her. 'Darling, please forgive me. I've been a stupid fool. I can't believe I left you on that island all on your own. It was such a crass and hurtful thing to do. Please say you'll forgive me. I'll do everything in my power to make it up to you. I'll even buy the damn island so we can go back there and have a proper holiday without me acting like a jerk and storming off as if work is the only thing I care about. I care about you. I love you.'

Abby could barely see through tears and threw her arms around his neck. 'Oh, Luke, of course I forgive you. I've ached to hear you say those three little words. I love you so much I'm just about bursting with it.'

He smiled at her with such tenderness her heart squeezed. 'You are the love of my life. I'm only half a person without you. Will you marry me and make me the happiest man on the planet?'

Abby choked back a happy sob. Could there have

been a more heartfelt proposal from a man in love? 'Oh, darling, of course I'll marry you. But what changed your mind? I thought you were—?'

'I'm ashamed of how I pushed you away when all I've ever wanted from the moment I met you was to hold you close. I love you, my darling. I think I've probably loved you from the first time you smiled at me.'

'I can't believe you just proposed to me in front of all these people,' Abby said, glancing at the assembled crowd outside her office cubicle, including Sabina, who was looking all dewy-eyed as if she'd been watching a romantic movie.

'I don't care who's watching,' Luke said. 'They can stream it live on Twitter or wherever else for all I care. I want everyone to know how much I love you.'

Abby hadn't thought it was possible to feel such happiness. Luke loved her. He wanted to marry her. It was a dream, a fairy tale come true. 'Ella is going to be beside herself. *I'm* beside myself.'

He stood up and then held her close. 'You're beside me and that's where you're going to stay for the rest of our lives.'

Abby stroked his face, her heart feeling so full when she saw the love shining in his gaze. 'I was so sad when you left me behind. But I realised when I got back to London I had to stop lying about how perfect my life was when it was anything but.'

He held one of her hands against the deep thud of his heart. 'I can't promise you a perfect life, I can't even promise to be a perfect partner but I can promise to love you and protect you for as long as we both shall live. Now, I think these people are waiting for us to seal this promise with a kiss.' His eyes glinted. 'Shall we get on with it?'

Abby smiled and lifted her mouth to his. 'Yes, please.'

EPILOGUE

One year later...

ABBY CAME OUT to the sun-warmed terrace at the villa on the island, where Luke was waiting for her to come back from the bathroom. *Their* island—Luke's and hers. Luke insisted it was his gift to her but he had already given her so much.

She hadn't thought it possible to be so happy and contented. They weren't a perfect couple by any means but their love for each other more than made up for that. Her lonely childhood felt so far away now. The love Luke showered her with more than compensated for the disadvantages she'd suffered as a child. Not a day went past without him telling her he loved her. He always said it first, not just when she said it to him. He showed it too in thousands of ways. Little things he did for her, like ignoring his phone when it rang when she was telling him something important, or even when she was telling him something unimportant. He made *her* feel important. He made her feel the most important person to him and that was something she was so grateful for.

Abby kept the pregnancy dipstick behind her back and came over to where he was sitting on a sun lounger with a book resting on his lap. 'What are you reading?' she said, leaning down to plant a kiss on his head.

He captured her by the hand and brought her down on to his lap, quickly shoving his book aside. 'Work stuff, but you're way more interesting.' He suddenly frowned. 'Hey, what's that you're hiding behind your back?'

Abby smiled and brought her hand from behind her to show him. 'Guess what? We're having a baby.'

Tears shone in his eyes and he swallowed deeply. 'Oh, darling, that's wonderful. I can't believe it. We're having a baby.' He gave a delighted laugh and gently cradled her head to kiss her. 'You'll be the most amazing mother, I'm sure of it.'

Abby looked lovingly into his eyes. 'And you will be an amazing father. I'm so proud of the way you've worked on your relationship with your dad since we got married.'

His broad smile warmed her heart. 'I know he's not perfect, nor ever likely to be anything close to it, but he's making an effort so the least I can do is make one too.'

Abby kissed him on the lips again. 'Maybe he'll make a much better grandfather than a father. Some people are like that.'

Luke stroked her cheek, his expression so full of

love it made her breath catch. 'You've taught me so much about relationships, my darling. You make me a better person. More understanding, more accepting, more forgiving.'

'You've taught me heaps too,' Abby said. 'Like how to be honest about what I want. And right now, I want you.'

Luke brought her mouth back down to his and gathered her close. 'Perfect, because I want you too.'

* * * * *

If you enjoyed Melanie Milburne's 75th book,
A VIRGIN FOR A VOW,
why not explore some more stories
by the same author?

THE TYCOON'S MARRIAGE DEAL
A RING FOR THE GREEK'S BABY
WEDDING NIGHT WITH HER ENEMY

Available now!

MILLS & BOON®

MODERN™

POWER, PASSION AND IRRESISTIBLE TEMPTATION

Just can't wait?
Buy our books online before they hit the shops!
www.millsandboon.co.uk

Also available as eBooks.

MILLS & BOON®

Coming next month

CLAIMING HIS NINE-MONTH CONSEQUENCE
Jennie Lucas

Ruby.

Pregnant.

Impossible. She couldn't be. They'd used protection.

He could still remember how he'd felt when he'd kissed her. When he'd heard her soft sigh of surrender. How she'd shuddered, crying out with pleasure in his arms. How he'd done the same.

And she'd been a virgin. He'd never been anyone's first lover. Ares had lost his virginity at eighteen, a relatively late age compared to his friends, but growing up as he had, he'd idealistically wanted to wait for love. And he had, until he'd fallen for a sexy French girl the summer after boarding school. It wasn't until summer ended that his father had gleefully revealed that Melice had actually been a prostitute, bought and paid for all the time. *I did it for your own good, boy. All that weak-minded yearning over love was getting on my nerves. Now you know what all women are after—money. You're welcome.*

Ares's bodyguard closed the car door behind him with a bang, causing him to jump.

"Sir? Are you there?"

Turning his attention back to his assistant on the phone, Ares said grimly, "Give me her phone number."

Two minutes later, as his driver pulled the sedan smoothly down the street, merging into Paris's evening traffic, Ares listened to the phone ring and ring. Why didn't Ruby answer?

When he'd left Star Valley, he'd thought he could forget her.

Instead, he'd endured four and a half months of painful celibacy, since his traitorous body didn't want any other woman. He couldn't forget the soft curves of Ruby's body, her sweet mouth like sin. She hadn't wanted his money. She'd been insulted by his offer. She'd told him never to call her again.

And now…

She was pregnant. With his baby.

He sat up straight as the phone was finally answered. "Hello?"

Continue reading
CLAIMING HIS NINE-MONTH
CONSEQUENCE
Jennie Lucas

Available next month
www.millsandboon.co.uk

LET'S TALK

Romance

For exclusive extracts, competitions
and special offers, find us online:

 facebook.com/millsandboon

@millsandboonuk

@millsandboon

Or get in touch on 0844 844 1351*

For all the latest titles coming soon, visit
millsandboon.co.uk/nextmonth